THE
KING'S PARK
IRREGULARS

AN ABIGAIL CRAIG MYSTERY

DAVID WILSON

First published 2012

The Mystery Press, an imprint of The History Press
The Mill, Brimscombe Port
Stroud, Gloucestershire, GL5 2QG
www.thehistorypress.co.uk

British Library Cataloguing in Publication Data.
A catalogue record for this book is available from the British Library.

ISBN 978 0 7524 6451 0

Typesetting and origination by The History Press
Manufacturing managed by Jellyfish Print Solutions Ltd
Printed in India

Chapter One

At eleven o'clock on a Monday morning in late July, Abigail Craig sat in a booth in The Burgh coffee shop watching the door for the arrival of her friend, Alasdair Mills, who would no doubt be running fashionably late as usual. Usually she was a creature of habit but since this particular coffee shop had only opened that very morning, it seemed like a good opportunity to try someplace new. Life can get stale if you don't try new things, she thought, and for one reason or another, well really only one reason in particular, she had not tried any new things this past year. She looked around, taking in the surroundings from her prime vantage point in the booth. It looked like most coffee shops with its welcoming, black, soft leather sofas and a row of stools along a bar in the window and at the back, opposite the counter, a row of booths where Abigail now sat. Just then she was distracted as a flustered man in an overcoat, black cords, shirt and a tartan waistcoat came through the doors and waved as he walked over towards her, 'Morning Abby, sorry I'm late. Had to get these flowers for Sophie.'

'You don't usually get flowers for her, which means you must either be in the dog house or up to something. Which is it?'

He threw his coat into the seat opposite and sighed heavily. 'The latter I'm afraid. I'll tell you about it in a minute, I need coffee first. What will you have?'

Abigail scanned the list of coffees along the back wall. 'I'll just have a regular coffee please.'

Alasdair raised his eyebrows. 'Come on Abby, it's an exciting time for coffee drinkers nowadays, why should the young have all the fun. I'm going to have a latte, with one of those fancy syrups. Can I tempt you? New coffee shop so a new you?'

'No thank you. I'm quite happy with the old me and my normal coffee.' Alasdair spun round and marched over to the counter to order the drinks with Abigail absently watching as he did so. At sixty-two he was only two years younger than she was but he could easily pass for being in his fifties. His greying hair was parted down one side and for his age he would still be considered handsome and, although his stomach had overtaken his chest in pushing out his waistcoat, his energy levels seemed undiminished. By comparison Abigail felt older these days than she should and her hair was almost completely grey, although thanks to her hairdresser it was always dyed over to keep up appearances, which was also aided with her smart clothes. Alasdair came back and slid into the other side of the booth and took a sip of his coffee. 'So, what do we think of the new place?' he asked, looking around. 'I like the touch of having these books here.' Along a shelf, which ran the length of the booths, were old sets of encyclopaedias which immediately drew Abigail's approval.

'Yes, I do like those. Anywhere there are books to read and especially for people to learn is always fine with me.'

'That's the head librarian talking but I agree, they are good.' They peered at the books which to them felt out of place here but at the same time also appropriate. Stirling was, after all, a university city and students were apt to have coffee from time to time, she was sure. They were not current but not so out of date as to be of little use and they were arranged neatly in alphabetical order, the spines displaying the subject with which each book started and finished. Alasdair pointed thoughtfully, 'Some of the contents seem quite intriguing,' he said. 'I take it these are where they start and end in the book.' Abigail scanned along the spines as well while Alasdair pulled a couple down. 'Look at this, *Chicago Death*, or this one with *Arctic Biosphere* and here's *Decorative Edison*.'

Abigail noticed two teenagers in the next booth reach up and take down one of the books.

'Look Alasdair,' she whispered, 'isn't that wonderful. It's lovely to see a thirst for knowledge in the young.' The two teenagers giggled and then replaced the book before sliding out of their booth and heading for the door. Curious about the laughter, Alasdair reached over and pulled the book out again, and, after reading the spine, held it up to Abigail who just sighed. '*Excretion Geometry*! I might have known.'

Alasdair laughed. 'A bit unfortunate if there's a practical exam for that subject!' he said, as Abigail's brow furrowed.

'Do you know I saw an article on breakfast television the other day. They said that in the next few years all reference books will be digitised and only available on the internet rather than being sold in book format. What do you make of that?' Alasdair frowned and shook his head, showing his disapproval. 'I mean what will that do for people's knowledge? If you look for information on the internet you're likely only to find out what you look for, and who knows who may have written it, but if you look it up in a book you might stumble on something on an adjacent page, or as you flick through the book, not to mention it having been checked over before it was published. It's very sad.' They sipped their coffees in silence for a moment, pondering the imminent downward spiral of general knowledge in society when Abigail remembered, 'Oh, so why are you in the dog house with Sophie?'

Alisdair heaved another sigh. 'Bit of a faux pas at a party yesterday and now she's peeved with me. It's my fault really although I blame her for letting me get the present.' Abigail was already starting to get the picture. Alasdair's wife Sophie was a saint and although he had retired a year or so ago she continued to work in her job in Human Resources in the Prudential just outside the city, leaving Alasdair to his own devices, which he used to try and embrace every possible notion that came into his head. She sipped her coffee waiting for him to continue.

'We were at a party for one of Sophie's work colleagues who was retiring, Bridget McAllister, a bit of a foul woman who was one of the supervisors. To be honest I think everyone was glad she was going. Anyway, Sophie was working to catch up with the new software system so she had asked me to go into town and get a present, then I was to meet her at the party afterwards in the Highland Hotel, which this Bridget woman had chosen. "No problem," I said, and since she had told me a bit about her I assumed I'd be on safe ground but it turns out I wasn't listening quite as closely as I maybe should have been.'

Abigail smiled. 'Imagine that. What did you do?'

'Well, I was running a little bit late and when I arrived they were just about to make the presentation so Sophie took the present off me and handed it over to Bridget in front of the assembled staff. But she seemed a little confused when she opened it.'

'What had you got for her?'

'Crampons.'

'Crampons! Those things for your boots when you're climbing?'

'Yes! Sophie gave me a look as if to ask "What on earth?" and I said, "You said that Bridget went climbing with friends so I though these would be handy." Sophie told me she'd said no such thing and Bridget was just looking at me as if I was a sandwich short of a picnic. Well, I suppose I wasn't thinking and I just blurted out what Sophie had said, 'No, you told me that Bridget was a social climber!' Well, you can imagine the rest.'

Abigail roared with laughter. 'Alasdair, you're a tonic. I can well imagine. It's a good job old Bridget was retiring!' She wiped the tears from her eyes, 'Sophie will let you off the hook later, she knows you well enough.'

Alasdair shrugged. 'True. By the way are you still remembering about the Collectors' Club meeting tonight?' Abigail unfortunately couldn't think of a good excuse to get out of it, although appreciated the thought of Alasdair trying to get her out of the house again and back socialising properly.

'Yes, seven thirty isn't it?'

'No, seven o'clock tonight since it's the first meeting in a couple of months, what with holidays and things. Why don't I swing by around quarter to and we can walk over to the Smith together and I can introduce you to everyone?' Abigail nodded and then slid out of the booth to put her coat on. 'Are you working today? How's the new girl getting on, the work experience one?'

'No, it's my day off today. She's fine although always seems to be distracted. I don't think working in the library was her first choice but we'll get there. She's young so maybe just needs to get used to working in the silence. I'm back in tomorrow.' They left a tip on the counter and then walked outside, 'Are you off home then, Alasdair?'

'No, I'm going to go into the Marches to see the carbon people.' Abigail looked confused. 'The who?'

'The carbon people from the council. They help you do your bit to save the planet, that type of thing. I've decided I'm going to go carbon neutral.'

'You're going carbon neutral?' Abigail stuttered. 'You do know that you'll need to make some sacrifices to do it and I'm sure that Mercedes you drive isn't a great friend to the environment.' So this is the new notion for this week, she thought a little despairingly, we'll see how long this one lasts.

Alasdair looked unphased. 'I don't think it'll be that difficult, now that the boffins have had a few years to work on all the technology I'm sure it'll be easy to make the changes without too much hardship. What's the cost to change a few light-bulbs?'

Abigail smiled. 'Ok, well good luck!'

Alasdair threw her a wave as he turned and marched off, as Abigail made her way up the hill in the opposite direction towards home.

Chapter Two

Alasdair strolled through the Marches shopping centre, as the crowd of morning shoppers were slowly blending into the gaggle of office workers racing around to do some SAS-style shopping (in and out in the minimal time and take no prisoners!) or pick up a sandwich for lunch. There seemed to be an unwritten rule that the mornings were for people of pensionable age to potter around but between eleven thirty and twelve those people should start to go home to make way for those who came out at lunchtime and were in a rush due to the need to return to their place of work. Alasdair watched as the younger men and women seemed to weave like grand prix drivers in and out of the last few remaining older people, although rather than being concerned with running off the race track they merely had to avoid clipping a tartan canvas shopping bag every now and again. Alasdair thought that he was in no man's land at this time since he was not actually of pensionable age, having taken early retirement from his law firm last year, but neither did he work. His role he felt was to be the buffer between the two, and to this end he would often find himself walking more slowly than he was capable, purely because he was aware of someone behind him on a mobile phone who wouldn't interrupt their conversation to say 'Excuse me', but would insist on trying to squeeze by anyway.

Just past the store, which had been the old Woolworths, there was a little stand in the middle of the floor, with a sign advertising the current push in the city to reduce your carbon footprint.

Alasdair approached the young woman, who was hovering around with a small handful of leaflets ready to leap out at passers-by.

'Good morning, young lady,' Alasdair was oblivious to her subtle stiffening at his address, 'I live in the city and I'm interested to do my bit.' The young woman, whose badge on her lapel stated she was called simply, Pamela, smiled at him.

'That's lovely, sir. It's always nice when people come to speak to us. So much of my day is spent chasing after people trying to give them leaflets that it's a nice change when someone comes to me. If I could only harness the energy I spend trying to catch people then I could power a small village!' She laughed at her own joke, and then stopped as Alasdair looked ready to walk off again, 'But anyway, can I ask what you do at the moment?'

'Well, I must confess that I don't really do much at all at the moment, however that's why I'm here. My wife and I do recycle of course but then these days you have no choice in the matter do you?' He raised his eyebrows as he said this, 'I mean if you don't recycle then you're very much frowned upon, it's the new parking in someone else's space, don't you think?' Pamela kept smiling, although an almost imperceptible wrinkle appeared on her forehead.

'Yes, sir, you do have to recycle but it's all for a good cause. The amount of waste that is needlessly dumped into landfill each year, each day in fact, is not good for our planet. We can all be so wasteful these days that I think it's nice to think twice about what can be used again. What about saving energy in the home?' Alasdair pondered for a moment.

'I'm not sure I can honestly say I'm doing anything on that front either. There's just my wife and I so we don't use too much energy, although Sophie does bake a lot for her committee meetings, and we do need to keep the house warm, and it's a big house even for the two of us.'

Pamela seized on this. 'Ah yes, sir, but have you considered that if it's only you and your wife then you could close the door on some rooms and only heat the ones you're using?'

'No, the trouble is you never know which room you might want to go into at any time of the day.'

'Ok, what about energy-saving light-bulbs?'

'No.'

'Solar heating?'

'No.'

'Or wind power?'

'No.'

'Recycling of water for the garden?'

'No. Unless our gardener does it, you'd have to ask him though.' Pamela's face changed slightly as a not unknown medical reflex came into play whereby the exact amount her smile faded was instantly replaced by the same amount of frown on her forehead. She knew there were a lot of people in Stirling doing fantastic work on the project, and she wondered how many of them were doing it to compensate for this one individual. But if I can change this one, she thought, that's like winning the World Cup. Alasdair was looking at the papers on the small desk, 'Good idea sir, why don't we have a seat and go through the energy survey and we can perhaps identify your needs.'

Twenty minutes later Pamela sat back, her hand throbbing slightly from the amount of writing she'd had to do in detailing where Alasdair was going wrong, and where he could start to put things right. 'It's not so much that you have a carbon footprint, Mr Mills,' she told him, 'It's more of a carbon crater.'

Alasdair glanced down the list. 'There are an awful lot of things on this list.'

'Yes it's not easy going Green, it takes a bit of effort but it pays off in the long run.'

Alasdair made a low ponderous noise. 'Perhaps what I need to do is not go the full hog and just go slightly Green. Maybe just to go Green light? That sounds like it would be the thing; after all, I'm not solely responsible for the state we're in. I could start a Green Light movement.'

Pamela smiled at him. 'Yes, but if you take all these things on board then just think how much future generations will have to thank you for.' Alasdair rose from his seat and folded the papers into his coat pocket, 'You do want future generations to have a good opinion of you, don't you Mr Mills?'

Alasdair forced a smile, looking around. 'I like to think I'll be remembered. Like Woolworths,' he said, 'I wasn't fully appreciated while I was here, but when I'm gone everyone will realise how good it was to have me around!' With that he strolled off, leaving Pamela to slump down in her seat and put the 'Closed' sign on top of the desk.

Chapter Three

As Alasdair was leaving the shopping centre, Abigail was turning the corner into her street in the King's Park area where she had lived for over twenty years. The King's Park is what estate agents would describe as being 'a highly desirable area' and in this case it would actually be true, consisting of street after tree-lined street of Victorian houses. The area had grown in the late nineteenth century when wealthy merchants and business people, buoyed by the prosperity of the Victorian age, moved to Stirling from Glasgow for a healthier lifestyle away from the smog-infested city. They would commute by train to and from work but enjoy living in the healthier surroundings of Stirling, something which has not much changed today in some respects. Albeit the trains are newer but the jury remains out on whether they are any better.

As she turned into the front path leading up to her semi-detached four-bedroom house, she was greeted by a ginger and white-coloured cat sitting on the doorstep looking up at her as she walked towards the door. It purred loudly as she stroked it behind the ear, 'Hello there. Who might you be?' She looked at the tag hanging from its collar, 'Aah, Waffles, nice to meet you.' She unlocked and opened the front door, trying to step over the cat, but as soon as the gap was big enough he padded in and wandered up the hallway with Abigail shouting after him, 'Waffles, come here! Bad cat! Come on out you go.' But the cat seemed oblivious to her calls and proceeded through the lounge door and out of sight from Abigail. She closed the door, stooping to pick up the post and, looking through the pile, tutted loudly on finding yet another plastic bag from a charity. It's not that she wasn't generous with donations to her charities but this was now the sixth bag waiting to be collected once it had been filled with old clothes. How many clothes do they think I have? If I could fill every one of these bags with clothes then I would have a bigger wardrobe than the Queen she thought as she placed the bag on the small shelf next to the door, causing them all to slide off onto the floor and making her tut loudly again.

Waffles the cat had made himself comfortable on an armchair, catching the sun as it shone in through the bay window. Abigail put a hand under his rump and tried to lever him off the chair but Waffles miaowed loudly and wouldn't budge an inch. 'Bothersome cat,' she muttered, as she went into the kitchen and switched on the kettle, and then returned to sit in the chair opposite Waffles, watching him relax in the warm sun. 'I think you're an old cat aren't you Waffles? You seem to have that look about you, and a distinct lack of get up and go.' She sighed, 'I know how you feel.' Her head drifted onto the back of the chair and she watched the trees outside the window sway in the gentle breeze. Waffles looked up and miaowed as the kettle clicked off in the kitchen and then he resumed his relaxed position. Abigail laughed to herself, 'You might as well have a cup of tea since you're as much at home here as I am by the look of you,' she stroked him on the head as she walked past to the kitchen. 'What a trusting cat. You must come from a good home to be this easy with people. Although once you get to our time of life there's not too much left worth fearing, is there Waffles?'

As she came back in with her cup of tea, she went back out into the hallway and looked at the small pile of plastic bags on the floor. Right, she said to herself, we need some sort of indexing system for those I think. If I'd let the library get into that state then we'd never find anything. She went upstairs to the large cupboard in one of her spare rooms, rooting around the boxes of Christmas decorations, cards, tinsel, and a holly wreath for the front door which she didn't know if she would bother putting up this year. Aah, here we are, perfect.

She went back downstairs and stood the green, plastic card tree against the wall just inside the front door. Down each side there were slots in which you could slide cards to display them rather than have them lined up along the fireplace. She slotted the charity bags into the tree in order of the days they had to go back out on the doorstep. There, she thought, standing back admiring her ingenuity, there's always a solution if you think about it. It won't get me on *Dragons' Den* but problem solved.

Once back down in the lounge, she sat down in her armchair again and enjoyed the heat from the sun which had moved round just enough to hit her chair as well. Five minutes and then you're going out, I'm sure your owners might be wondering where you are. But five minutes came and went as Abigail's eyes closed and she drifted into a sound sleep, with a gentle purring from the cat the only sound in the house.

Chapter Four

Alasdair Mills' wife, Sophie, checked herself over in the bedroom mirror, adjusting her grey woollen jumper and smoothing down her dark trousers. Her short blonde hair had been carefully brushed and minimal make-up applied just to show willing. After all, the other members of the Stirling Community Planning Committee were generally a reserved bunch and as she was trying to organise the biggest event in their history she wanted to appear in every way respectable and in command of the job. She came downstairs to find Alasdair sitting on the sofa gazing at a pair of tatty old slippers on the table in front of him. 'Still trying to come to terms with the fact that you paid eight thousand pounds for those flea-bitten things?'

Alasdair looked at her. 'These are not flea-bitten things as you well know, and they were worth every penny!' He picked them up gently and put them back inside the glass display case which he had ordered to be specially made for them and which would have pride of place in his study bookcase very shortly. The slippers had once belonged to Sir Walter Scott and as Alasdair had a passion for collecting everything he could to do with the man, when these had come up for auction a few weeks ago he had decided he must have them for his collection. He knew they would cost him a tidy sum since they were highly prized by Walter Scott collectors, and the museum at Abbotsford, Scott's former home, wanted them badly as well. But Alasdair had held his nerve and outbid everyone else for them and not without a huge air of satisfaction had he posed for a photograph in the paper to make sure other collectors could see that he had been victorious. As far as he was concerned this was the crowning glory on his collection of first editions and other items – a pair of slippers once owned and, who knows, perhaps even once worn by the great man himself as he wrote.

Sophie was getting organised, 'Are you remembering I've got my committee meeting tonight?' He nonchalantly picked up the newspaper as if not really interested.

'Yes. Do you want me to come along to lend a hand?' he said, trying again to hide his peevishness at never having been invited to attend the Stirling Community Planning Committee despite his status as a respected local solicitor, now retired of course.

'No thanks, I think you've done enough to help me out already, don't you?'

He looked hurt. 'Why, what have I done?'

'You know very well this is the last meeting before the big day on Sunday and I've got to keep everyone on side and make sure things are organised. That's difficult enough but as you well know Bridget McAllister will be there and I'm not exactly her favourite person at the moment.' He lifted his newspaper and rustled it into shape.

'She shouldn't be so touchy. Anyway, I've got a Collectors' Club meeting tonight at the Smith. I've persuaded Abby to come along and see if she likes it.'

Sophie sat down next to Alasdair. 'How is she doing? I've not seen her much recently what with being so busy with the organising committee.'

Alasdair lowered the paper again. 'I think she's fine, although she seems like a shadow of who she used to be. It's like the winds just died from her sails.'

'I hoped she would be picking herself up again by now, it's been nearly a year since Arthur died.'

Alasdair smiled at her. 'But when you're married that long it takes a long time to even start getting over it, if you ever do. She mentioned she'd been looking through Arthur's stamp collection and had found a list of stamps he was missing to complete it and she might try to find them. I think she felt it would just be a nice thing to do for him since he can't do it himself now.'

'That's nice, might help her to move on. Is there anyone at the club that can help her with it?'

'Yes, Bruce is a stamp man so he'll hopefully be able to give her some pointers. Arthur was quite the philatelist and his collection is quite impressive; he showed it to me a few years ago when he used to work on it in the office at lunch. Well, we'll see how she goes. I think it might just do her good to get out and about again. She's as tough as old boots really, she'll be fine.'

Sophie kissed him on the cheek. 'It's just not true what everyone says about you is it?' a wry smile forming on her lips. 'You're quite a considerate soul after all.' She got up before he could reply, 'I'm going to head off, see you later.' She disappeared out of the lounge door, picking up her coat and shoulder bag as she went, leaving Alasdair to gaze wistfully at his famous slippers, his face a picture of pride and joy.

Alasdair was organised and leaving the house fifteen minutes later to walk round to Abigail's house, which was only five minutes away, as he and Sophie also lived in the King's Park. He turned right at the end of his garden path and walked up the street, past a white works van parked at the road, although no one was inside. 'That's the trouble with these old houses,' he thought, 'always something going wrong with them.'

At Abigail's house he knocked on the door and waited to see the frosted shape of Abigail through the glass coming to let him in, but she never appeared. This time he gave the door a louder knock and bent down to the letterbox, 'Abby! Come on, tick tock tick tock!' He heard movement inside and let the letterbox go with a metallic crack as it closed.

A few moments later Abigail opened the door and was about to chide him for making such a racket but before she could, a ginger fur ball came racing down the hall and out through Alasdair's legs nearly knocking him off balance. 'Good God Abby! What the hell was that?'

'That was Waffles, and I didn't think he had that amount of energy in him. He's been keeping me company this afternoon.' She watched as he ran over the road and then came to a sudden stop, clearly deciding it was now time to wash. 'He's fast for an old cat.' Alasdair closed the door behind him.

'Where did he come from? He's not yours is he?'

Abigail glanced back. 'What if he is?' She didn't wait for a reply, 'But no, he just appeared on the doorstep and then made himself at home. He was on a five-minute warning but I fell asleep in my chair, the heat from the sun just knocked us both out. I've never seen him before, so I think he's maybe new to the area. I'll not be a moment and then we can go.' She started walking up the stairs as Alasdair went into the lounge.

'Can't cats sense when people are unhappy or in need of company?' he shouted up after her, 'I think it's an inbuilt thing they have. Or is that dolphins? I think it might be dolphins, Abby.' The bathroom door closing upstairs cut him off and he carried on the discussion in his own head.

The lounge was a traditional Victorian style, with a large bay window and a feature fireplace with a black cast-iron fire and sturdy mahogany surround. The wall around the fire was painted the Victorian red that Alasdair thought should be written into the title deeds if you were buying one of these houses; that and you must always have your outer front door painted black, and it must always have a holly wreath on it during December. The suite was a leather Chesterfield style, and along the opposite wall from the fire there was a large, dark wooden sideboard. Alasdair plodded around the room while he waited, looking out at the pleasant evening, and then, walking past the sideboard, he stopped as he noticed all of the photographs that had been strewn across the top. She's been wandering down memory lane again, he thought as he picked through some of them. They ranged from Arthur and Abigail's wedding day, at which Alasdair was the best man and looking quite dapper in the photographs, to them walking out on their honeymoon, to the birth of their son Charlie. 'Happy times,' he mused as Abigail walked in and found him looking at the pictures.

She just smiled. 'I thought I'd do a bit of tidying but I didn't get very far. It's amazing how you can lose time in your memories.' Alasdair smiled.

'We'd be lost without them. Wasn't it Charlie's fortieth this year?'

'Yes, last month. He asked if I wanted to go over and stay with them for a while but I don't think the Florida sun would be good for me nowadays.'

'Be just what you need, Abby, a nice holiday and some proper sunshine.'

'Maybe. Anyway, we should get going. So how many people do you think there'll be at the meeting?'

Alasdair let out a thoughtful sigh. 'Difficult to say really, I'm hoping for a good turnout. Our numbers had dwindled a little by the last meeting in May, but we all agreed to have a recruitment drive while we had our break so could be a big turnout. We had best get going and not keep them all waiting!'

Chapter Five

The Smith Art Gallery stands on Albert Place and is an imposing
building with Greek-style pillars on its façade, and a pedestrian
area out front adorned with flags and banners advertising the
current exhibition on 'Rugs of the Reformation', one of the
gallery's more obscure offerings. Inside, the foyer led past the
enquiries desk and beyond to the gallery rooms where the
main exhibitions were housed, and beyond that the permanent
collection of various Scottish and local artefacts. Namely, several
to do with the social history of the area, quite a few to do with
William Wallace and Robert the Bruce, and the pride and joy of
the Smith, the oldest football in the world. Standing in front of
this particular exhibit was a twenty-five-year-old man, wearing
jeans and a zip-up casual top, and a tidy head of mousy brown
hair. Bruce Dickson stood quietly gazing at the football, waiting
patiently for the last ten minutes before the Stirling Collectors'
Club meeting began. He was lost in a daydream when a member
of staff from the gallery stood next to him, 'Amazing isn't it?'
Bruce looked around suddenly, 'I'm sorry; I didn't mean to give
you a start. I just thought you might be thinking how amazing it
is that we have something that's the oldest in the world?'

Bruce stammered a reply. 'No, I was just looking. I mean yes,
it is.'

'Do you like football? I'm quite a fan, Stirling Albion you
understand, so more of a masochistic thing than anything else but

you've got to support your local team, don't you think? Anyway, it always impresses me that we've got this here.' Bruce looked at the football again.

'I suppose, I'm not really a sports fan. I prefer watching movies to sports.'

The man looked at him curiously. 'Not *any* sports? You must like at least one, even if it's something daft like shinty or tiddlywinks?

'No, not really.'

'Ok, but you must still admit that it's amazing we've got this here. It was found in the castle and dates back to the fifteen hundreds you know. They found it up in the rafters in Mary Queen of Scots' bedroom. I mean, how did it get there? I used to get hell from my parents playing football in the garden, never mind in the bedroom. I bet someone was having a fly kick about while Mary was off somewhere else and then had to scarper. It probably wasn't the done thing to knock on the door later and say, 'Sorry your Majesty, can we have our ball back?'

Bruce gave a weak smile. 'I suppose not,' he said as the man puffed his cheeks out, clearly finding this was like pulling teeth and deciding to move onto someone else. Bruce, glad that his enforced sociableness had ended, wandered back through to the small room off the foyer where they had laid out around twenty chairs for the meeting, all of which were empty apart from the one now occupied by Bruce himself. How am I going to explain this to Alasdair, he thought as he looked around the empty chairs, he'll not be happy.

As Bruce was sitting in the empty room at the Smith, Sophie Mills was taking her seat at a table in the small room set aside at the council offices for their meeting tonight. The members of the Stirling Community Planning Committee were taking their seats while the chairperson for tonight, who much to Sophie's dismay was Bridget McAllister, brought everyone to order, 'If you can all settle down please we can begin.' She had a voice like an old school mistress and spoke down to everyone as if they were her pupils. Sophie smiled in her direction hoping to thaw the freeze that had been evident when she entered the room, but this was met with an icy scowl that seemed to suggest that permafrost had set in. 'If I can have your attention please,' Bridget shouted down the table, 'I'd like to bring this meeting of the High Tea in the Park organising committee to order.'

High Tea in the Park had been Sophie's brainchild, much to Bridget's disgust, and was inspired by the pop festival which took place every year in Perthshire; however this one was a little more civilised and hence, High Tea in the Park. With the event only six days away Sophie had everything planned with military precision, despite attempts by her husband to help her. She felt very protective about this part of her life since Alasdair was used to being involved in various things when he was a solicitor and now this was her turn and she wasn't going to let him barge in. High Tea in the Park would take place in the King's Park where the large grass events area would play host to a stage where classical musicians would play through the afternoon and into the evening, and two large marquees would serve high teas all through the event, with proceeds going to local charities. When Sophie had first proposed the idea it had been met with some scepticism but Sophie had thought it through quite carefully. The timing of the event near the end of July was key, since a lot of performers and orchestras were in Scotland already for the Edinburgh Festival starting in early August and, just as Sophie had predicted, they jumped at the chance to use this event to have a warm up and try out new pieces of music on the public. On top of that, as everyone agreed, who doesn't like a high tea? Toast to start, then a nice main course and tea and cakes to finish. It was lovely, and time it was given the status again that it once had as it was certainly a very civilised way to spend some time while enjoying the excellent music.

Sophie spread her notebook out on the table and looked to Bridget to hand over the floor to her so that she could go over the final points. Bridget glowered over in her direction and nodded her head and Sophie smiled at the rest of the group.

'Good evening everyone, and thank you Bridget. I'm glad you could all come tonight. I'm pleased to say that I have had confirmation back from the Helsinki Fiddle Orchestra that they will be able to attend,' this met with nods of approval as they were highly regarded, 'and also the Paris Flugelhorn Orchestra have said they can do an hour for us in the evening so I thought they might be a good lead up to the fireworks at ten o'clock to close the event?' Again, nods of approval all round, with Peter Finchburgh, an elderly gentleman held in good esteem in the committee, holding up his teacup in salute.

'Well done Sophie, jolly good show. This is going to be a belter!' A cough from the top of the table drew everyone's attention as Bridget gave them a sardonic smile.

'I think you'll find we do have some issues to resolve, far be it for me to dim Mrs Mills' moment in the spotlight.' Sophie was determined to be the bigger person.

'No problem Bridget, fire away.'

'We have a letter of concern from a local resident, who feels the bouncy castle is somewhat inappropriate.' Bridget passed the letter down the table to Peter Finchburgh, who scanned over it while Sophie looked confused.

'What do they mean? It's just a bouncy castle for the kids. We cover it in white sheeting to look like icing and then place a space hopper on top to look like a cherry. Surely someone can't complain about that?'

Peter stroked his chin as he read. 'Blah blah blah . . . have concerns that the bouncy castle has the appearance of a large breast and is not in keeping with the tone of the area let alone the event. Hah! What a load of nonsense!' He threw the letter down on the table. Sophie picked it up and read it over as well.

'Bridget, don't you stay in the same street as this person?'

'Yes, she's a neighbour of mine, but I don't see what that has to do with it.' Sophie was about to say something she might regret when someone else chipped in.

'Well, we should take a vote and see if the committee requires a change. All those in favour of the current proposal, say Aye.' A chorus of 'Aye' went up from the table, which brought a smile to Sophie's face and a deepening scowl to Bridget's. 'Thank you all,' Sophie said. 'What a relief! So, Bridget is there anything else?' Bridget shook her head and Sophie breathed a calming sigh as Bridget got up from the table.

'Oh, sorry Mrs Mills, I forgot to mention. The Provost has had to cancel due to a family illness, so you have no guest of honour to do the opening and closing addresses. Dear me, you'll never find a suitable replacement at this stage.' The smug expression on Bridget's face nearly made Sophie get up and go for her, but she bit her tongue.

'You couldn't have mentioned this sooner? When did you find out?'

'Oh, he called me first thing this morning. I would have been in touch but I know you're very busy so I thought it could wait until tonight.'

'Yes giving me even less time to find a replacement.' Peter Finchburgh banged the table with his fist.

'Nonsense Sophie, we'll find someone else to do it. There are plenty of upstanding people we can ask.' He turned to Bridget; 'That's a bit mean Bridget, waiting to tell us about that. You've given us a mountain to climb now.' As soon as he said it, there was a stifled snigger around the table, causing Bridget to gasp in a breath of air.

'I think it's just. . .' she stammered.

'No,' Peter came back, 'we're not going to lose our foothold on things here, and we'll still make sure we peak at the right time. If need be we'll hold a further summit tomorrow to sort this out.' The stifled sniggers grew to a laugh with Sophie just amazed at the outburst. Bridget threw them all a scowl and then marched out of the room, the sound of laughter following her into the corridor.

Sophie tried to quieten them down. 'Stop it! You'll get me hung with old Bridget. How did you all know anyway?'

'Oh, you can't keep a secret around here; a man from the Pru told us!'

Chapter Six

Alasdair skipped up the steps of the Smith Art Gallery with Abigail following behind, 'I think I can hear a crowd inside Abby, we're in for a busy night!' Abigail herself couldn't hear any such crowd but assumed Alasdair must have more highly attuned hearing than she did. They walked through the foyer and turned the corner into the small ante room just off and Alasdair stopped dead in his tracks, catching Abigail off guard and nearly causing her to walk into the back of him. Bruce looked up and gave a weak smile as Alasdair surveyed the rows of empty chairs. 'Where is everyone?' he asked.

Bruce shrugged his shoulders. 'This is it I'm afraid, and I just came to tell you the news. We've started another club, on Facebook.' He glanced towards Abigail, assuming an introduction would be forthcoming, but Alasdair was having a palpitation.

'Another club? How can you start another club, there's only one Stirling Collectors' Club. What's this Facebook thing anyway?'

Abigail tutted behind him. 'For goodness sake Alasdair, don't you keep up with anything? It's a website where people can meet and become friends and share their interests from anywhere in the world.'

He looked at her and then turned to Bruce again. 'Are you sure? *Everyone* has joined your new group?'

'Yes. I tweeted everyone yesterday to let them know there was a meeting here but they were much happier with the Facebook club. They were, apparently, finding it a little too limiting just speaking to each other here so we've linked up with collectors in other parts of the country and even some overseas. It's the future, much more opportunity.'

'Tweeted?' Alasdair's mouth was agape.

'That's right.' Bruce's face flushed. 'I tweeted them. You know, on Twitter.'

'Is that, may I ask, a website for twits?'

'Erm, no. It's just a way of keeping in touch on the internet. People add you to their list and everyone can see what you're thinking each time you post a new message.'

Alasdair turned to Abigail again. 'Have you heard of this?'

'Oh yes, it's all the rage at the moment. We have the computers in the library for people to access the internet and people are always coming in to check their Facebook pages or to update their Twitters. It's just the modern way – you can even do it on your phone now if I recall?' She looked towards Bruce for confirmation.

'That's right it's quite easy, look.' He took his phone out of his pocket and was about to get up when Alasdair, who had started pacing around in front of the chairs, erupted.

'We don't want to know how to do it Bruce! This is outrageous, they can't just start another club and abandon this one. Right, I'm going to have a word with them about this.' He stormed off outside to phone a few of the other members, as Abigail sat down.

'It's Bruce isn't it? I'm Abigail Craig, a friend of Alasdair and his wife.' Bruce smiled, 'I came along to join the club and meet some new people but there don't seem to be any. Apart from you of course, although I think Alasdair was expecting a much bigger turnout.'

Bruce shrugged again. 'It's nothing personal, we just decided that while there were no meetings we might be as well to meet online and it's turned out to be quite good so no one felt it was worth coming back.'

'I see. It seems to have come as somewhat of a shock to Alasdair, although I suppose things do move on don't they? *Tomorrow's World* always told us days like this would come, although I think only the compact disc really took off the way they said it would. No jetpacks in sight yet in any case.' Abigail could sense Bruce was not the least bit relaxed. 'What is it that you collect Bruce?'

'Well stamps mainly, although I've branched out into anything to do with films and television.'

'Oh? Such as?'

'Posters, props, autographs – that type of thing.' Abigail waited for the usual reciprocal question, which never came, so she offered the information anyway.

'That sounds interesting. I'm just starting out in collecting. It's stamps for me too, although the collection belongs to my husband,' she caught herself, '*Belonged* I should say. He died and I had a look through and found a list of stamps he wanted to get hold of and decided it might be nice to try and finish it for him. We'll see. Although if we've now disbanded then I'll need to go elsewhere, maybe even on this Facebook.'

Bruce grimaced. 'Don't let Alasdair hear you say that.'

'No, perhaps not,' Abigail laughed. 'I suppose I can see why you've started it. It won't be much fun for your generation hanging around with us old fogies when everything is done on the internet nowadays. It was decent that you came here tonight.'

'I just thought someone should come and tell Alasdair in person about it, that's still the fair way to give someone bad news.' Abigail put a finger to her lips as Alasdair came back in. Alasdair sat down and threw his arms in the air, 'It's true. They've jumped ship and gone into hyperspace.'

'I think you mean cyberspace,' Bruce offered.

'It doesn't really matter, they've deserted me. It's like a cull. *Et tu* Bruce,' he said, glowering at Bruce menacingly, although Bruce did not appear to be overly concerned.

Sophie Mills was poring over the local paper when Alasdair got home, flipping through the pages scanning each one. Alasdair slumped down into his chair, 'You won't believe what happened tonight. Treason of the highest order at the club; we've been decimated to only two members, and that's me and Abby. Can you believe it?' Sophie didn't respond, 'Sophie?'

She glanced up. 'Sorry I wasn't quite listening, yes, terrible news. I'm afraid I've got a big problem for Sunday.' She explained what had happened at her committee meeting, 'I'm hoping there'll be someone in the newspaper that I can contact to act as guest of honour.'

'I'm sure you might find someone in there who's held a position of some respect in the community, and is regarded as somewhat of an elder statesman in the city. Although it may be difficult to get them on such short notice.'

Sophie kept scanning the paper. 'Well, I have to try. We can't have a . . .' she glanced up at him. He was smiling at her innocently. 'Obviously we thought of you immediately Alasdair but since you're married to the person organising the event it might look a bit improper if you were suddenly thrust into such a position. After all, we wouldn't want any scandal or impropriety would we, not with your good name in the community?'

He nodded. 'I suppose not. It is a fine line to walk when you're a man of my position.' Sophie lowered her head to the paper again, rolling her eyes as she did so.

'It certainly is,' she said.

Alasdair wandered off towards his study when Sophie shouted after him, 'By the way, you left the back door open when you went out. I had to close it when I came in, it was freezing in here.'

He stopped. 'But I wasn't at the back door, it must have been you.'

'I wasn't out there either! You're getting forgetful in your retirement, but you can't go out leaving the doors open.'

He carried on out of the lounge towards his study, 'It's not me who's forgetful,' he muttered, 'I didn't leave the door open. Must have been you, too much of a hurry that's the trouble. I wouldn't have been a very good solicitor if I just forgot about things here and there!' He walked into his study and went to have a look at his slippers to calm him down, stopping dead as he noticed the empty glass case. 'Sophie!' he yelled, waiting for her to come through.

'What is it? There's no need to shout.'

He pointed towards the glass case. 'Did you move the slippers?'

'No, I wouldn't dream of touching those things. Are you sure you put them back again?'

He looked around the study desperately. 'Of course I did but they're not here now. You must have . . . oh hell,' he noticed his wastepaper basket had been kicked over and a large boot print on one of the sheets of paper on the floor. 'We didn't forget to close the back door. We've been burgled!'

Chapter Seven

At seven thirty on Tuesday morning Emma Harris carefully zipped up the holdall which contained as many of her clothes and possessions as she could carry, and put it down by the front door. She looked down the hallway of the flat which, for the last two years and for the next five minutes, she shared with her husband. They had known each other for just over the two years and had been married for the last eighteen months. Her family had told her she was marrying too quickly, that he wasn't quite the right one for her and she should wait but, being twenty-one and determined to go her own way, she had married John at a Registry Office wedding and then had moved to Stirling to live with him in his flat. If only I had listened to them, she thought; still, I suppose we all have to live and learn. Things had started off well enough but then he had started behaving a little strangely, working long hours, unexplained gaps in what he was doing. He was either having an affair or was being systematically abducted by aliens. As it turned out the former was correct. Even then her stubborn streak wouldn't let her leave him and the rift between her and her family became a gulf.

They say that once a cheat always a cheat, and yes there may be the odd exception but it seemed to her that John was happy to be typecast. After catching him out a week ago with some text messages on his phone, and after a good few blazing arguments and sleepless nights since, she had decided that for her own sanity she had to leave. She just hadn't told John about her plans.

The last thing she needed before she could leave was her mobile phone. She cursed herself for leaving it lying on the fireplace in the lounge where John was sleeping on the couch. I don't know how he can sleep so soundly, she thought, maybe he's nothing to feel guilty about? No, more like it that he just doesn't care. Creeping quietly through the room she stalked her phone, carefully sliding it off the fireplace and putting it into her pocket. Turning around to leave, she stopped to have a last look at her husband. I could leave you a note I suppose or even do the decent thing and wake you and tell you face to face but I really don't think you deserve that level of consideration. You've certainly not shown me any so, no, you sleep on and when you wake up you can do what the hell you like.

With that she walked back out of the room along the hall and, picking up her bag on the way out, drew the door closed quietly behind her.

Abigail always made a point of getting to the library early before anyone else arrived, as she loved the complete silence inside. She pushed open the heavy wooden door, locking it behind her and then took the few steps up to the lending library where she glanced around at the rows of books. As part of her morning routine she went upstairs to the reference section, which was her favourite part of the library. The smell from all the antiquated books just seemed to hit her on a primal level and she sometimes enjoyed sitting up here after the library was closed, just reading through some of these old volumes. Since Arthur had died she had never been in much of a hurry to go back to an empty house so this gave her a nice escape from the loneliness of home. As the other staff arrived, the library slowly came to life and they all set about the business of the day. Abigail had been a librarian

for many years and had watched some of the visitors grow up –
not only in years, she had seen their level of reading grow with
them too. People who came in as children and borrowed their
first books, developed to the teenage novels, then perhaps to
educational books and then inevitably they might move upstairs
to the reference library when they were working on projects for
college or university. Abigail found that she had a unique position
to have a window on some people's lives depending on which
books they borrowed. You could get a feel for people from the
type of fiction they read, or the people who took out travel
books, and then those that took out self-help books to try to
address some problem they may be facing. Whatever you needed
to know in life, it was in the library, although nowadays many
people would just Google it and not bother with the library at all.
What will we do when there are no more libraries, she thought;
we'll be in a predicament then, I can tell you.

Abigail was tidying through the reserved books shelf when
her work experience trainee Emma Harris came in and pushed
a large holdall under the counter. She gave Abigail a brief smile
and Abigail smiled back, 'Morning Emma, how are you?' Then
pointing to the holdall she said, 'Are you staying for the week?'

Emma smiled nervously. 'Oh fine, no just a few things to take to
the charity shop later. Thought I might pop round at lunchtime.'
Then she grabbed a pile of books from the counter and headed
to the shelves, clearly keen to avoid any further discussion on the
subject. Abigail watched her as she worked and she seemed her
usual distracted way, but today something was different. Abigail
didn't know her that well, but there seemed to be the weight of
the world on her shoulders today.

Emma's mind was racing as she beavered about the library, scarcely
believing that she had walked out on her home, such as it was, and
her life. How could I have been so stupid, she thought, where

am I going to go? I can't live on the streets and I can't go to my family. I can't bear a large chorus of 'we told you so'. By half past eleven she couldn't take any more. She felt claustrophobic in the library, the silence seeming to just let her thoughts shout even louder in her head. She grabbed her coat and shouted over to Abigail, 'Just taking an early lunch, won't be long.'

Abigail raised her head from the computer to reply, but Emma was already on her way out of the door. Valerie Stewart, one of the other librarians, came over and stood next to Abigail.

'She's not going to last long here, Abby, if she keeps doing things like this. She was late three times last week as well, which is not the sign of someone who wants the work experience!'

Abigail pondered for a moment. 'There's something not quite right with her.'

'You can say that again,' Valerie snorted and then she was off putting more books back on shelves. Abigail went over to one of the windows and watched Emma head over to the park benches on the hill leading to the Albert Halls and slump down onto one of them, her head in her hands.

Chapter Eight

Police Constable Chris Buchan looked around as he waited outside the elegant Victorian house for someone to answer the door. His gaze travelled along the houses across the road and he noticed an old woman waving at him, so he waved back. She shook her head and gestured him to come over, but as he was pondering this the door opened behind him and he was faced by an angry-looking man, 'Good morning sir, are you Mr Mills?'

Alasdair leaned out and looked up and down the street, 'Where's everyone else? They haven't just sent you have they?'

'Yes, sir. May I come in?' Alasdair was glowering at him as he opened up the door and waved him in.

'What about forensics, where are they? And what about CID, I assume they'll be coming?' PC Buchan waited in the hall to be shown where to go, since there were several doors leading off.

'No, sir. I'm here to take a statement and have a look at the scene. From the information we received when you called last night it sounds like a common burglary so we won't need forensics. They're very busy today with a murder in any case.' He watched as Alasdair walked ahead into the lounge, muttering over his shoulder as he went.

'The last thing this is, young man, is a common burglary as you put it! Did they tell you what has actually happened? I know that you people are not always the most effective at these things.'

'Us people, sir?'

'Yes, the police. I know very well why they've only sent one person. I doubt if there's much credit to be had in following up what you think is a simple burglary, but this could be the making of your career. Reputations have been secured in solving crimes such as this, like the man that tracked down the Great Train Robbers, look at him, or Jack the Ripper.'

'I don't think they ever caught Jack the Ripper, sir.'

'Exactly! I rest my case.'

PC Buchan was about to answer when a woman entered and Alasdair greeted her in an exaggerated gesture, 'Ah Sophie, there you are. This is the cavalry in the form of . . . what was your name?'

'PC Buchan.' Sophie smiled at him, introduced herself and offered him a seat. She seemed much more reasonable and he sensed he should make her the focus of his enquires. He declined a cup of tea, feeling the weight of Alasdair's stare on him.

'If you could explain to me what happened and what items have gone missing?' He listened and jotted down some notes of the facts from Sophie as Alasdair paced around behind the sofa she was sitting on. 'So the only items stolen were a pair of slippers?'

'They were not just any old slippers,' Alasdair said, his face aghast, 'these slippers were a part of our national history and once belonged to Sir Walter Scott.'

PC Buchan didn't look overly impressed. 'I see.'

'But do you see, young man? They were bought only a few weeks ago at a price of eight thousand pounds! Not exactly a common item to be stolen in a common burglary, wouldn't you say?'

PC Buchan nodded slowly. 'I suppose that's true. So to be clear, sir, you paid eight thousand pounds for a pair of slippers? I mean for the antiques?'

Before Alasdair could launch into another outburst, Sophie stepped in quickly. 'Perhaps if we show you the back door where they came in and also the study from where the items were taken?' She led him through to the kitchen and he had a look at the door.

'It does seem to have been opened quite skilfully,' he said. 'No crowbar marks or signs of force. They must have opened it with the lock. Does anyone else have a key?' Sophie shook her head.

'No, there's just myself and my husband. Our son has a key but he lives in America.'

PC Buchan examined the lock. 'It's quite an old lock; you might want to get it changed. It wouldn't have taken much to open this.' He stood up again. 'If I can have a look at the study now?' Sophie led him through the house to the study, with Alasdair following behind, his foul mood not helping in the least.

Alasdair strode over to his bookcase,. 'There you are, the scene of the crime. I kept them in this glass case, it has specially treated glass to keep the sunlight from harming them.' PC Buchan noted this down, hoping that his involuntary eye rolling had not been seen. I wish I had money to waste on stuff like this, he thought, eight grand for slippers and keeping them in a glass case. He noted down a description of the case and the slippers, 'So nothing else was taken? Any drawers or cupboards opened or ransacked?' Sophie shook her head, 'Have you checked all of your jewellery Mrs Mills?'

She nodded. 'Yes, all accounted for. It seems they haven't touched anything except the slippers. Oh, and the waste-paper basket. They must have kicked it over and there's a footprint on this piece of paper.' PC Buchan stooped down to look at it, humming thoughtfully, 'It doesn't look muddy, and there weren't any other footprints by the back door?'

Alasdair shook his head. 'What exactly does that tell you?'

'Well Mr Mills, it was raining yesterday evening and if the burglar had come in at that time I would have expected there to be some footprints evident near the back door at the very least. Since this looks clean, they must have come in before the rain, which suggests to me they must have known you were out and took their opportunity.'

Alasdair looked unimpressed. 'How do you come to that conclusion?' PC Buchan gave a sigh which he should have regretted, but he couldn't help himself.

'Because Mrs Mills told me before that you only went out around half past six. It was still daylight at that time and the rain only came on later in the evening. So the burglar must have come in and out during daylight, which suggests some confidence in their ability. Wouldn't you agree? It doesn't suggest some opportunistic night prowler. That and the fact they only took the slippers suggests it was an intended break-in for the slippers in particular.' Alasdair grudgingly agreed and although keeping it well hidden, he now had some small amount of respect for the young officer. PC Buchan walked back out of the study and down to the entrance hall, 'I have as much as I need for now Mr and Mrs Mills. Given the circumstances I think it might be a good idea if we do have our forensic team come by to check for fingerprints and remove the paper with the footprint. If you would be so kind as to stay out of the study until they've been and avoid touching the back door any further that would increase our chances of finding something.' Sophie thanked him for his help, while Alasdair said nothing, and she showed PC Buchan out of the front door.

Sophie came back in to find Alasdair pacing around the lounge.

'I don't know why I paid my taxes all these years Sophie. One police officer, for a crime of this magnitude! I ask you.'

She put a hand on his arm. 'Calm down. He was very good and he did say he'll get forensics to come out to look for, whatever it is they look for.'

'Clues perhaps?' Alasdair said sarcastically.

Sophie fixed him with a glare. 'I don't think having an attitude with me will help the situation, do you?' He said nothing and sat down knowing that he was in danger of getting the sharp end of her tongue, 'I'll get us a cup of tea,' she said, 'in fact maybe a nice stiff drink would be better. This is all very upsetting knowing someone was in our home.'

Chapter Nine

'So here you are?' Emma jerked her head up, startled by the unexpected voice, but it was Abigail standing over her, smiling, 'May I sit down?'

Emma quickly wiped away the tears that had been running down her cheeks. 'Erm . . . yeah, if you want to.' Emma shuffled along to the end of the bench and Abigail sat down, and placed the plastic box she had been carrying on her lap, 'I thought I'd take an early lunch too and I saw you over here and thought we might have lunch together. We've never done that, but it's quite nice to have someone to have lunch with, don't you think?'

Emma looked at her, bewildered. 'I suppose so, although I don't have anything with me, I just needed some fresh air.'

'I have more sandwiches than I need, here, take one of mine. They're just ham salad but I made them myself, none of the shop bought things that you can get. I always find those so expensive, don't you? And how they get away with calling that stuff ham is beyond me, you'd think the EU would have something to say; they seem to have something to say on everything else, don't they?' Abigail thought Emma might refuse her hospitality, but she picked up a sandwich and thanked her and then started to eat it, as Abigail did likewise. The sun was shining down through the trees, and the warmth hit them both, as they just sat and gazed out over the grass with the statue of Rob Roy standing over them, his sword held aloft. Emma glanced towards Abigail, who had her face turned up to the sun and her eyes closed, enjoying the heat on her face. Hesitantly she said, 'I've left my husband. This morning I packed my bag and just left.'

Abigail opened her eyes and then put the lid on her lunchbox. 'Can I ask why?'

'Cheating. I found out he was cheating on me, yet again, and I couldn't take it any more. Now I don't know what to do as I've got nowhere to go. I feel so stupid, I'm going to have to go back home tonight, unpack my bag and then start again and he'll have won, again. It's like I'm stuck there.'

'Don't you have any family or friends you could go to?'

Emma sighed. 'No, my family were against this from the start and I took John's side and didn't keep in contact with them, and much the same story with my friends. I thought he would be the only one I needed, but it turns out that was a load of crap. Stupid.'

Abigail turned to face her. 'No Emma, not stupid. Maybe unwise but then none of us know everything, we all have to live and learn. I'm sure your family would understand though, wouldn't they?'

'I don't know, I said some horrible things and it's been so long. I can't go to them now after that. I'll just need to bear it, it's my bed and I'll need to lie in it.'

'You could do that, but then how many other women will also be lying in that bed when you're not there?' Emma looked at Abigail, tears again running down her face. Abigail put a hand over hers, 'I've not had the experience you've had. I was married for forty years to a wonderful man and I miss him like mad. There's no reason you shouldn't have that as well, and if you start again now you could, my goodness you're so young. I've not met this John, but one thing I know is you never realise the damage people like him are doing to you until it's too late. They're like lead poisoning Emma, you don't notice it happening but they slowly kill you and by the time you discover it, then it's too late.' Emma rested her elbow on the arm of the bench and put her head in her hand, and Abigail could see her shaking, holding back the emotions going on inside her.

'I'll need to try and find someplace to go, maybe there's a women's refuge or something I can go to until I can sort myself out.'

Abigail thought for a moment. 'I think they're usually for women who've been abused. Might be difficult to get into one of those, but I do have another suggestion.' Emma looked over at her hopefully. 'You could come and stay with me. I've plenty of room and there's just me so it would be nice to have the company.'

Emma shook her head. 'No, I couldn't, it's too much. I couldn't just come and stay with you, you don't even really know me.'

'No, but we'd soon change that, and you'd get to know me as well. You never know, you might find me to be terrible to live with!' Emma said nothing, but Abigail could see in her eyes she was torn trying to decide what to do, 'Come on, even if it's only for tonight, at least it gives you time to think what you're going to do.'

Emma nodded and smiled. 'Thank you.'

Abigail stood up before she could say any more. 'No need to thank me, it'll be good. Now, I don't think you're in any state to work the rest of today so I'm going to fetch your holdall and we'll go and get you settled in. Miss Stewart can manage for the rest of the day, which will do her good!'

Chapter Ten

Emma laid her holdall on the bed in Abigail's spare room and sat down next to it, looking around and taking in the décor. It was a reasonable size, like most rooms in Victorian houses, and had been decorated with green and white large-print wallpaper on one wall, which also had a black cast-iron fireplace and mahogany surround. The curtains were carefully picked to complement the wallpaper, as were the covers on the bed. Emma noted that the bed was a queen size and there was no duvet, but it was dressed with sheets and a heavy bedspread. The debate would rage on for ever and a day about which was better, but at this time, Emma just recalled that this was what she had when she was young, when things were good and easy, and the memory comforted her. There was a light knock on the door, and Abigail's voice drifted through, 'Emma, I've got the kettle on if you like, I thought a nice cup of tea might be in order?'

'That would be great, thank you. I'll be down in a moment.' Emma stood up and looked out of the window to the front of the house, the street outside lined with trees, and the similar properties over the road. This is how life should be, she thought, maybe there is hope for me yet if I can get my act together. Well, maybe.

As Emma walked into the lounge, with its large bay window and traditional furniture, Abigail was setting down a tray on the coffee table with a pot of tea, two mugs and two custard tarts. She sat down on the couch as Abigail took what was her usual chair at the side of the fire, and poured them each a mug of tea. Abigail handed Emma her mug and a plate with a tart. 'Sorry it's not the proper teacups, I just find these much easier and I find them more comforting. A bit more homely, I always think tea cups are for formal occasions.'

'That's fine, did you make the tarts yourself?'

'I did, an old recipe of my mother's which I find still hasn't been bettered. Where do your parents stay?' Although Abigail was a tactful and thoughtful person, there were times when it was better to just ask. People were sometimes a little taken aback, but you could waste an awful lot of time skirting around things.

Emma sipped her tea, looking out of the window. 'Glasgow. At least that's where they were the last time I was in touch with them. It's been a while.'

'What brought you through here?'

Emma shifted a little in her seat and her face flushed slightly. 'John worked here when I met him and I moved in with him after we were married. My mum said it was a mistake and I would regret it and things seemed to escalate from there. We had a big bust up and, well, the rest is history.'

Abigail sat back in her chair. 'Quite. But the question really is what you choose to do with the future?'

'I'm not sure how many choices I have at the moment to be honest. I've no money behind me, and I'm not sure where I go from here.'

'Nonsense!' The sudden rise in Abigail's tone of voice startled Emma, 'You've got it all to play for now, and today could be the most important day of your life. You shouldn't underestimate what you've done today – you've decided that you're not going to let someone else dictate the course of your life and you've taken back control. As far as I can see, the future could be whatever you want to make it.'

Emma put her mug down and walked over to the window, standing with her back to Abigail. 'It doesn't feel like it. I mean I don't know where I can go, what I can do with my life . . .'

'These are all things that can be worked out later my dear, for now you just need to take some time and sort yourself out and, without trying to sound too Oprah, find out who you are again. You're most welcome to stay here as long as you want. I've plenty of room and it's very handy for work as well, and you'd be helping me out too.' Emma turned around as Abigail had risen from her chair and picked up a photograph from the sideboard and handed it to her. It was a photograph of a young woman in her wedding dress, and next to her was a handsome man in a three-piece suit, both beaming at the camera. 'That's my Arthur and me on our wedding day, fourteenth of August nineteen sixty four. I was nineteen and he was twenty-two and we both just knew when we met that we were meant to be together, we could just feel it. We were married for over forty years, until he died of a heart attack last year. It's like losing a piece of yourself when you lose someone after that long together, but you have to try to pick up the pieces and go on as best you can. Maybe we're both heading down similar roads.'

Emma put the photograph back on the sideboard. 'Maybe.'

They sat back down in their seats and sipped their tea for a moment, before Abigail laid her head back on her chair, gazing thoughtfully at the ceiling.

'I remember my mother telling me of one of the mottos they had during the war, since things were in short supply you couldn't just replace clothes or household things. You had to "make do and mend", and maybe that's what we need to do now. Things might not be the same for either of us, for different reasons, but we must make do and mend.' She smiled thoughtfully and tea was drunk in silent contemplation.

Chapter Eleven

The forensic team came earlier than expected and Alasdair watched as they dusted the back door and then in and around the study to check for fingerprints. 'Don't you normally wear blue paper suits for your work?' he asked. The lead member of the forensic team kept working. 'Not for this type of job, sir.'

Alasdair had calmed down quite a bit by now and was secretly enjoying the fact that he had a forensic team on his case. 'I see you're like the American's on the television then, they never wear the blue suits at all when they visit a crime scene. I've seen them on *CSI* wherever and they just go in and solve crimes straightaway. Not like they do on *Lewis* or *Morse*, where they always have the blue suits on. Are we less careful over here and need to take extra precautions?' The forensics man stood up and faced Alasdair.

'Those programmes are full of nonsense,' he said gruffly. 'We do the job right and when we need to we put on the blue suits. It's standard procedure. I'm surprised most of the people in those shows aren't in prison what with the amount of forensics they must leave behind them! Big bouncy hair and sporty training shoes, lovely to find traces of those but not if they belong to you. Now if you don't mind sir, we won't be too much longer.' Alasdair retreated to the lounge and waited for them to finish.

After they were gone, he wandered around the house unsure what to be up to. He found the loss of his beloved slippers quite unsettling and couldn't find the patience to sit down to read or watch television. He went into the kitchen where Sophie was sitting at the table, 'Aren't your work expecting you in today at all?' he asked.

'No, I told them I'd have to take the whole day off. They were fine; they know it's quite an ordeal dealing with a break-in and the police and everything. Besides, I can use the time to try and find our new guest of honour for Sunday. I can't believe we're in this situation. I've advertised us having a guest of honour and it just knocks everything off if we don't have one.'

Alasdair opened and closed the cupboards around the kitchen. 'Can't you just do it, or what about old Bridget, ask her? That'll make her happy again.' He proceeded to open the fridge now.

'I'm not asking her to do it, she'd love that. I could do it but it's not quite the same as having a guest of honour, besides I'll be too busy on the day running things.' She looked up, distracted by the doors opening and closing. 'What are you doing? I'm trying to concentrate.'

He sighed. 'I'm not sure, just knocks you for six when something like this happens. I can't settle.'

'Maybe you could go and be unsettled somewhere else so I can think about this?' He picked up a sheaf of papers from the end of the worktop, his list of items from the carbon neutral people, and skimmed over them.

'Maybe I'll go out and see how much some of these things cost. Might as well do something to kill the afternoon. Do you want anything?'

'No thanks.' Alasdair put on his jacket and stepped outside the house, surveying the street to see if there was anyone he could tell about his dramatic event, but unfortunately there wasn't. However as he was about to start walking, a movement across the road caught his eye. It was his neighbour, Dorothy Grey, waving at him from her bay window to beckon him over.

He walked over the road to her house and being that there was no doorbell, raised his hand to knock on the door. As he did so, the door opened a crack and Dorothy Grey's small curious face looked through at him, 'Oh come in, please.' The door opened further and the small, grey-haired woman was smiling at him and gesturing him into the hallway, 'I saw you coming out of the house and thought I should try and talk to you about your incident. I obviously spoke to the police as well and they seemed interested in what I saw, but I thought it would be good to tell you also if the chance presented itself. As you may know I don't go out much, but my armchair faces out of the window so I do sometimes see what happens in the street. It's just unavoidable. Would you like a cup of tea?' She closed the door and walked briskly past Alasdair into the lounge with him following behind, suddenly feeling old compared to the apparent energy this elderly woman had. She motioned him into a chair and then disappeared into the kitchen, and a moment later her bright face peered back round the door at him, 'I'm sorry Mr Mills, I don't think you know my name, we've never really chatted. It's Dorothy, like in *The Wizard of Oz* and Grey, like the Earl.'

He did know her name but it was true they had never really chatted. He thought it funny that here were two people who had lived across from each other for years and the only things they knew of each other were what they heard from others. Then again, he thought, there were some families that were like that so it's not so surprising I suppose. Her head disappeared again and Alasdair rose from his chair to follow her into the kitchen. The room was warm from the Aga, which was nestled in between some free-standing units that looked like they had been there since before the war. A small round table and one chair sat in front of the window, and scattered across it were various components of a Sunday newspaper.

She noticed him glancing around, 'I'm sorry it's such a mess,' quite oblivious to the fact that it was in fact very tidy. 'It takes me all week to read the Sunday paper, although I do like the articles in the magazines, usually very interesting. It keeps the brain active, along with books as well of course. I don't have a television you see, so I do read an awful lot. I used to have a television, but when the picture went I never bothered to replace it. Do you have a television, Mr Mills?'

'Absolutely,' he replied, 'I must have it for the news and the documentaries; I like to keep up with what's happening in the world.'

She beamed at him. 'I quite agree, I find the internet very good for that. It's my one concession to technology, after the telephone of course – we must keep our window on the world,' she chuckled, 'as well as my window on the street!' She smiled at him, and then bustled past him with a tray on which rested a teapot in the shape of a cat preparing to pounce, and two cups of which the handles were small mice hanging off the rim. Alasdair followed her in and they sat down. She's as batty as anyone I've ever met, he thought, watching as she poured the tea – nice, but batty. He took a cup from her and settled back into the chair, 'So the police already spoke to you did they? I didn't have much faith in them at all; I didn't think they were taking it very seriously. Not impressed.' He scowled into his tea, remembering his conversation with the officer who had taken their statement.

Dorothy considered this for a moment. 'I can understand that you might think that. After all, when it's a crime being committed against oneself you never think the police are doing enough. But the police officer did seem very attentive, and he was at your house for some time. I assume that was the forensic team who called this afternoon? Did they find any clues?' Alasdair mumbled that they might have been there long enough but they didn't turn up any clues or evidence. 'Ah, so it must have been a professional job,' she sipped her tea thoughtfully, 'perhaps someone you've offended in some way or a competing collector for those slippers? I remember it being in the newspapers that they had been sold at auction; the paper gave you a small mention with your photograph so anyone would know where to find them I suppose.'

'I hadn't considered that, although I should have thought about it beforehand. Hindsight and all that. You mentioned that you had told the police something interesting?' She put her cup down and her face took on a conspiratorial expression and her voice hushed to a whisper.

'Well, Mr Mills, I was sitting in my chair listening to the evening play on the radio, when I noticed a van pull up outside your house. I thought, you'll not get any answer there, since I had seen both you and your wife go out earlier. I was sitting in my chair a while you see, one can't help but notice things. Two men got out of the van, and instead of going to the front door, they immediately went straight round the path to the back of the house.'

Alasdair raised his eyebrows. 'Really? I saw a van parked further up the road when I went out last night but no one was in it.'

'Did you notice the name on the side?' He shook his head, a little annoyed that it might have been important and he hadn't noticed. But then why would I, he thought, since at that time I didn't know I was about to be burgled.

'So the men went round the back of the house?' he asked

'Indeed they did, and they were carrying a bag with them, which I assumed must contain tools to do a job you had hired them to do. The sign on the side of the van was,' she pulled a small notebook out from the side of her cushion and flicked through it, 'Castle Roofing.'

'You took a note of it? That's quite a clever idea.'

She smiled at him. 'First rule of neighbourhood watch Mr Mills, take note of anything out of the ordinary. If it turns out to be nothing then so much the better, but you never know. Anyway . . .' Alasdair was frowning, which stopped her mid-sentence.

'But why did you think someone coming to look at our roof was out of the ordinary? It seems fairly ordinary to me.'

'True, but this was a small van, and you have a large house on which the roof is quite a climb,' she raised her eyebrows expectantly for him to fill in the blank but the only blank was his expression, 'They had no ladders Mr Mills.' Alasdair felt stupid for not guessing it.

'Of course, so did you see anything else?'

'No, not really, they were out of sight for roughly,' she consulted her notebook, 'eight minutes, and then they came back out and drove off. I didn't think any more about it until I saw the police this morning and I wondered what had happened. I managed to attract the attention of that delightful PC Buchan as he was leaving your house and he came over to speak to me.'

Alasdair finished his tea and placed the cup down, rising to leave. 'Well, thank you Mrs Grey, you've been very helpful. I wonder why he didn't come back and mention this to me before he left.' She now blushed ever so slightly.

'I gather he didn't feel you were particularly receptive to the police.'

Alasdair puffed himself up indignantly. 'I would have been more receptive if they'd had something to tell me.'

Dorothy smiled at him again. 'But they did you see, but you weren't receptive to hear it. If I may say Mr Mills, and forgive me for paraphrasing from your Mr Walter Scott whom I'm sure you know better than I, but generally, attitude is equally as important for success as ability.' Alasdair frowned and then turned to leave. 'Mr Mills, perhaps this may be helpful,' he turned and she handed him a small page from her notebook.

'What is it?' he asked.

'That is the registration number for the van. I wrote it down too just in case. I gave it to the police; you should have it too so you're up to speed with us.' She smiled and wished him a pleasant afternoon as he went off up the street, with a little flea in his ear!

Chapter Twelve

The afternoon passed uneventfully as afternoons often do and Abigail and Emma had sat and talked for a while. Abigail noticed that Emma looked very tired. 'Perhaps you should take a lie down? Maybe a nap?'

'If that's OK I think I will,' she replied, 'I didn't sleep at all last night and I just feel drained.' Emma went up to the guest room, undressed and slid into bed. The chill from the fresh sheets was soon replaced by the warm comfort of the blankets and she drifted off.

In the lounge Abigail went over to the sideboard and picked up a photograph album and returned with it to her armchair. She opened it and flicked through the pages, the photographs of her wedding day and she and Arthur on their honeymoon in Blackpool bringing back vivid memories. That was back in the day when Blackpool was the place to go, she thought, no money for foreign holidays back then and thankfully no hen or stag parties in Blackpool. At least not ones like people have there now, all noise and cocktails. She sat back and allowed the memories to wander through her mind, remembering them fondly as she drifted off into the latest in a long line of afternoon naps.

Abigail woke with a start, with the clock saying it was five fifteen, and Emma's voice drifting down the stairs. Her tone was defiant which Abigail took to mean it was her hopefully now ex-husband she was speaking to. She put the photograph album back on the sideboard and went to the kitchen to prepare something for dinner. Emma appeared a few moments later, 'Anything I can do to help?'

Abigail was putting some leftover casserole into the oven. 'No thanks dear, this just needs heated through. How are you feeling, everything OK?'

Emma's face was still a mix of stress, anger and worry. 'I've no idea to be honest. That was John on the phone, demanding that I come home straightaway.'

'Oh? That doesn't sound like a man filled with regret.'

'No. I think he's angrier about the fact that I might have left him, rather than the fact that I'm gone. You know what I mean?'

Abigail pondered it for a moment. 'Yes, and that just says to me that you're making the right decision. Maybe I'm a little biased because it's nice to have company in the house again. But the real question has to be if you feel that you're doing the right thing?'

Emma raised her eyebrows and exhaled a puff of air. 'I don't think I could go back now even if I wanted to. I feel terrified by the thought of what I've done, but at the same time I can't help feeling relieved and a little excited as well. I'm really grateful to you for taking me in but don't worry I won't stay long, I just need to figure out somewhere to go.'

Abigail waved her hand to dismiss the notion. 'Oh, I'm quite glad to help and you can stay as long as you want. The old place has felt quite empty since Arthur passed on. This house just wraps me like a warm blanket and keeps me safe so there's no reason it can't do the same for you if you let it. As I said before, you're a lot stronger than you think. I'm sure you'll do fine.'

'I hope you're right,' she smiled, 'and I hope you'll be fine too?'

'Oh, I know I'll be fine. I lost a big part of me when Arthur died, but I remember him saying to me once that if he went first I was to think of our life together like a really good book. "You'll be sad for a while that you've finished it," he said, "because you loved it while you were reading it. But then you remember all of the exciting things that were in it and they make you smile."'

'That sounds like a nice way to think of it.' The phone ringing interrupted them and Abigail went to the hall to answer it, returning a minute or so later.

'That was my friend Alasdair Mills, he and his wife were burgled last night.'

'That's terrible, are they both OK? Did they lose much?'

'They're both fine, just Alasdair's antique slippers were stolen. The police think they may have been broken into specifically for those since nothing else was taken.'

Emma raised her eyebrows. 'He has antique slippers?'

'Oh yes, they once belonged to Sir Walter Scott. Cost him eight thousand pounds at an auction not so long ago.' Emma's face looked shocked, 'You'd understand if you met him. I've said I'll go round after dinner to see them, since Alasdair likes to make a crisis out of a drama. You can come if you like, might be good to get out and have some civilised company for a change?' Abigail realised what she'd said, 'Not that you don't have civilised company. I'm sure you do, I just meant . . .'

Emma smiled. 'I know what you meant, don't worry. Although I'm not sure if I'm up to being sociable.'

Abigail smiled this time. 'I understand. Well the offer's there if you want to and maybe some of my casserole will give you a boost. I can guarantee that an evening with Alasdair will take your mind off your troubles!'

Chapter Thirteen

Having been unable to persuade Emma to accompany her, Abigail walked around the corner a little after six thirty to visit Alasdair. The weather had turned and there was a light drizzle but the clouds looked foreboding, suggesting they could unload their contents at any moment. As she approached the Mills' garden path, Sophie was just coming out of the front door. 'Hi Abby, how's things? I take it you heard our news?'

'Yes, how are you? It must have been a shock, it's a terrible thing people coming into your house like that.'

'Oh, I'm fine. I was a little shaken up, not that you-know-who noticed since he's in mourning for his slippers. But we've had a locksmith round today to put better locks on the doors so we're all secure again. I think its a little easier knowing they seem to have come for the slippers rather than it being a normal break-in.'

Abigail nodded. 'I suppose that's true, although what an awful business coming to your house for those.'

'I know, and they were tatty old things as well. I guess there's no accounting for taste! But with the break-in and the problems with the high tea event I'm just about run ragged.' Sophie explained the problem with the guest of honour pulling out at almost the last minute, 'Don't suppose you've any suggestions have you? Or even better anyone you know who we could ask? I'm just off to a brain-storming session with the committee and my mind is more of a breeze at the moment than a storm.'

Abigail shook her head. 'Not that I can think of from the top of my head, but if I can come up with anyone I'll let you know.'

'Thanks Abby. Anyway, I better dash, he's in the study I think, just go in and shout through. There's a supply of G and T in the drinks cabinet!'

Alasdair was pacing around his study gazing sorrowfully at the empty glass case on the bookcase, when Abigail's voice wafted through the house. 'I'm in here Abby,' he shouted back, 'come through.' A moment later Abigail appeared in the doorway holding a glass with a gin and tonic she had prepared on the way past. 'Thanks for coming Abby, it's been a trying day.'

Abigail nodded sympathetically. 'I can imagine. I saw Sophie on the way out, it must have been a shock for her too.'

'Well, yes, I suppose. Although it's me that's lost one of our national treasures; what are people going to say about that. It's my reputation which could lie in tatters if this gets out.'

Abigail looked over at the glass case. 'So that's where they were taken from is it?'

'Yes, no leads from the police of course. The forensic people were here this afternoon but they didn't find any fingerprints on the case. They must have been wearing gloves.'

Abigail frowned. 'I'd be surprised if they could find anything in this gloom. Why is it so dark in here?'

'Oh, I've kept the curtains closed, for security and to keep any press photographers out. You can't be too careful with the paparazzi you know.'

Abigail walked over to the desk. 'Yes, maybe, but you could put another lamp on so we can see what we're doing!' She switched on the desk lamp, which grew from a small point of light into a very dim glow hardly throwing any light around the room at all, 'There must be something wrong with this one.' She strode over to the other side of the room and a small side table on which stood another lamp which she switched on, with much the same effect as the first one.

'This one isn't working either, maybe it's your wiring, these old houses can be funny at times that way. I'll switch on the main light.' She walked to the door and flicked the switch, which resulted in yet another dim glow emanating from within the light shade hanging from the ceiling.

Abigail looked at Alasdair. 'What on earth? What's happened to your lights, have the bulbs gone?'

Alasdair slumped into his chair. 'No, the bulbs were new today. It's the carbon people to blame on this one Abby.' Abigail took a seat, having a feeling there was a story about to come forth.

'Who?' she asked.

'The carbon people at the council, you know – the ones I saw in the Marches yesterday? It's my new energy-saving light-bulbs. I'm helping to save the environment you know.'

Abigail rolled her eyes. 'That may be, but it won't do much good for our sight trying to peer through this gloom. What wattage did you get? These new low-energy light-bulbs are better than they used to be, they shouldn't be this bad.'

'It's not that simple Abby,' he said, bringing out his energy report from a drawer and placing it on the desk. 'The carbon people ran a check on my carbon footprint and told me it was a bit of a monster. They gave me a list of things I should be doing to try and cut my energy use so I've taken them on board.'

'So, it was the energy-saving people who told you to keep your house lit like a cave? I don't think they count light pollution as part of the problem, you could surely have better bulbs than this?'

Alasdair looked deflated. 'Yes, but when they told me all of the things I should be doing, like changing my car, new glazing, walking more than driving, avoiding flying, it all seemed a bit draconian! I mean they can't seriously expect me to take the bus, I've seen some of the people who take the bus and I don't think it would be for me.'

Abigail exhaled. 'Excuse me Mr high and mighty, but I use the bus sometimes and I'm quite sure it's safe and the people on it are fine too. So if you've to do all these things, then what does that have to do with these awful bulbs?'

Alasdair leaned over, looking pleased with himself. 'Well, I read somewhere about governments who make agreements to offset their carbon emissions, so I did a little research and decided that I'm going to do that as well. It's fantastic. The carbon people said that I should use 60-watt energy-saving bulbs. But what I thought was, if I use 20-watt bulbs then I can offset that against taking the bus!' His face broke into the satisfied smile of someone who has outwitted the system.

Abigail looked slightly confused. 'But Alasdair, the amount of energy you save by using the lower-watt bulbs won't make much of a dent against your Mercedes. You'd need to be doing a lot more to offset that, wouldn't you? And what about when you fly abroad for holidays? That uses up a lot of your carbon allowance so you'll never be able to offset that, unless you're going to holiday at home.'

He looked shocked. 'I can't holiday at home. I need to get away to the sun, it's good for me.'

'Then you need to start embracing some of the things on this list, don't you?'

Alasdair sighed again. 'But there's so much to do, it's not easy all this Green stuff.'

Abigail tossed the list back onto the desk. 'If it was easy then everyone would be doing it and we wouldn't have a problem with any of this.'

'True I suppose,' he put his feet up on the desk, 'I'll need to have a better look into all of this business. Anyway Abby, what do you think we can do about this burglary? It's very frustrating waiting around for the police to come up with something.'

'It's only been one day! Have some patience for goodness sake.' Abigail sipped her drink, 'What seems to be a more important issue at the moment is Sophie's problem finding a new guest of honour. You must have some thoughts on that don't you?'

Alasdair threw up his arms. 'I've offered Abby but to no avail, she says it might look biased. Some of these celebrities want paid thousands, which is out of the question on her budget, and Sophie's keen to get someone local to kick things off, since it's the first one. I mean who can she ask here?' They sat for a time and thought about this before moving on to other topics, including the subject of Abigail's new lodger. 'Do you think it's wise, leaving her with the run of your house while you're out? She might be a con artist and while you're gone she and this husband of hers will be clearing out your house.' The thought had crossed Abigail's mind but ultimately she had to trust her judgement and her feeling was that Emma was genuine.

'We could go through life thinking that about people, Alasdair, but I know her and I'm pretty sure she's fine. The world would be in a terrible state if we couldn't help out a fellow human being in need, wouldn't it?'

Alasdair nodded. 'Yes, but just be careful that's all I'm saying. These people can tell if someone's vulnerable and they seek them out to prey on them.'

Abigail stiffened and looked annoyed. 'Where do you get this idea I'm vulnerable and can be "preyed upon" as you put it? You make me sound like I'm incapable!'

'Steady on Abby, I'm not suggesting that, it's just that it's not been long since Arthur died and you might . . .'

She cut him off. 'I'm well aware of that, although it's a pity you didn't show the same concern to him when he was alive and who knows what would have been. If he hadn't been worked into the ground when you decided to sell off your share of the business then he might not have had his heart attack.' Abigail regretted saying it as soon as the words left her mouth and she knew really it wasn't down to Alasdair. But there had just been a few too many comments about her fragile state and it had started to irk her. When Arthur and he had been in partnership they were very close friends but when Alasdair decided to take early retirement and sell off his share of their solicitors practice, it left a huge burden on Arthur to keep on top of things. It was worse that Alasdair sold out to a larger chain of solicitors, one of those companies who carry out property conveyancing on the 'stack them high and sell them cheap' philosophy. Arthur's problem was that he was just too involved and cared so much about his business, his staff and customers that he couldn't seem to extricate himself from it, until the matter was taken out of his hands and into those of a somewhat higher authority.

Alasdair stood up and marched from behind his desk, 'I think perhaps we should call it a night Abigail, before we both say something we'll really regret.' His tone was restrained but angry. 'If you really think I'm to blame for what happened then just come out and say it, but I can tell you you'd be wrong and I'm quite sure you know it! Let me show you out . . .' He opened the study door and gestured her in the direction of the hall, at which Abigail strode out of the room, picking up her coat on the way, and left without another word.

Chapter Fourteen

Abigail stormed in her front door, letting it slam loudly behind her. The walk around the corner had been too short to calm her down, although in truth she was angrier with herself more than anything else. Emma's voice shouted through from the kitchen, 'Abigail? I've got the kettle on if you'd like a cup?'

'No thanks, think I need something a little stronger if you'd care to join me?' Emma appeared from the kitchen as Abigail was pouring two glasses of gin and tonic.

'Everything alright?' Abigail handed Emma a drink and they sat down in front of the fire which was barely glowing in the hearth.

'Oh, I just had a bit of a fall out with that old . . .' her voice trailed off since she was never one to bad mouth anyone if she could help it. 'Daft really though, I think he just hit a nerve. You know how sometimes you can be fretting over something within yourself but when someone else puts their finger on it, it annoys you? It's like it was something you didn't have to admit to anyone else but it turns out someone's noticed it anyway and the cat's out of the bag.'

Emma nodded. 'I suppose so. What was it he said?' Abigail got up and threw another log onto the fire and stabbed at the embers.

'He said I was vulnerable and not really myself, and he put it down to Arthur's death.' She gazed into the flames as they started to grow steadily, 'The trouble is though, he's right.'

Emma gave a dismissive wave. 'You seem fine to me, in fact considering how recently it happened I'd say you seem remarkably fine. Men always think there's some reason we act irrationally – if it's not our time of the month, it's our hormones, or our time of life, or just that we're women!'

Abigail laughed and sat back down. 'You could have something there,' she took a long slow sip of her drink, 'but the annoying thing is he *was* right. The world seems a slightly scarier place now I have to face it alone. Arthur and I were a team, we met the world head on and nothing would phase us. Now I seem to be creeping around trying to stay under the radar and just play at things now. I go to work, I come home, and I go to work . . . I feel like I've thrown in the towel and I'm too young for that. I shouldn't have said what I said to him though. He was only trying to help and I lashed out because he was right and I didn't want to accept it.' Abigail explained to Emma about the conversation with Alasdair, refilling their drinks as she did. Emma listened, which Abigail liked; she didn't try to jump in with meaningless comments, but just listened and took in what she was hearing. 'Anyway, it'll all blow over I'm sure.'

Emma looked at her and nodded. 'I'm sure it will. Maybe getting a little bit angry was what you needed, to feel what it's like to have the blood running through your veins again?'

'Maybe so. I certainly owe Alasdair an apology now though, which will make him insufferable!' she laughed. 'But if it wasn't for friends like he and Sophie, and now you too, I'd been in a sorry old state.' Abigail held up her glass and Emma did likewise, 'To friends old and new, and to new beginnings.'

Emma smiled. 'I'll drink to that. I've had an eventful night myself.'

'Oh?'

'Yes, I had about twenty missed calls from John and a few choice voicemails as well. You can imagine. I called him back and told him to stop calling me and then I told him exactly what I thought of him and that he was on his own. I believe he may have used some expletives but as I was ending the call I didn't quite have the pleasure of catching them. He really is an amazing prat.'

Abigail put a hand over Emma's. 'Well done. How do you feel?'

She sighed. 'I feel relieved more than anything. I suppose I'm like you in that it felt good to feel my heart thumping in my chest as I spoke to him but this time it felt different. I wasn't the one being trodden over, I felt like I had grown to about ten feet tall.' They finished the rest of their drinks and then Emma got up and poured two more.

'Sorry Abigail, I didn't ask, do you want another one? I just have a feeling I'll sleep better if my brain's a little less active.'

Abigail nodded. 'Sounds fine to me. It's been a while since I've had a good few drinks, it'll do me good as well.' Emma sat back down on the couch and they both watched the fire for a few minutes, just savouring the quiet, the comfort, and the thought of new beginnings.

Emma glanced across. 'Abigail . . .?'

'Hmm . . .?'

'Something else I need to tell you. I might be leaving the library.'

Abigail sat up and looked at her. 'Why? Don't you like it?'

'I do, it's been great but . . .' she tried to put it into words, 'it's just not really me. I only took the job for the work experience to try and get me back into a job, and as much as I've enjoyed working there with you and some of the others, I just find it a bit too quiet.'

Abigail looked surprised. 'I always find it quite a stimulating place to work, although I've worked there for years. I think it's a place that gets into your soul over time. What do you think you'll do?' Emma's eyes lit up.

'Well, after I'd had the run-in with John I felt I needed some fresh air so I went for a walk and ended up in the town. There's a new restaurant opening up soon in King Street and the owner had a sign in the window for an assistant manager so I just went in to find out about it and I've got an interview tomorrow.'

Abigail raised an eyebrow. 'Assistant manager in a restaurant? Have you any experience in that sort of work? I'm no expert but it can be a demanding job working in these places.'

'No, although I did help out in a sandwich bar for a summer job when I was a teenager; it was called Give us Piece, not a big place but quite well liked by people. Anyway I just wanted to do this. I might not get it, I'm sure there are lots of people going after it, but I just had to go for it. It was a spur of the moment thing but it felt like I was destined to walk in there, and if I hadn't had the break with John and been living here, then I would never have been walking tonight and seen it. It's funny how sometimes things can work out. We'll see what happens. You're not annoyed are you? I am grateful for the job you gave me, but . . .'

Abigail smiled, quite warmly. 'It's fine. In fact it's nice to see you this excited. It reminds me when I started in the library as a trainee, my parents thought it was a bit of a waste but I just knew I wanted to do it. Sometimes you have to follow your heart rather than your head.' She got up and stoked the fire again, making the flames jump up and cast a warm glow over the room, 'I think perhaps one more drink before I turn in, how about you?'

'Perfect.'

Sophie Mills came home to find Alasdair sitting in his chair nursing a glass of malt and watching a repeat of *Colditz* on the television. 'You look cheery, what's up with you?' Alasdair relayed the evening's events with Abigail and Sophie plumped herself down next to him on the sofa. 'I wouldn't worry too much, Abigail will calm down and realise you were trying to help. It sounds a bit rash to me as well, taking in this lodger, although she has always been a very good judge of character, I'll say that for Abigail. It'll all blow over.'

Alasdair shrugged. 'I don't know, she seemed quite annoyed, not like herself at all. She's usually quite calm about things.'

'Maybe she isn't quite herself, but she shouldn't be trying to suggest you had anything to do with Arthur, it was his own fault. He had the chance to sell his share as well after the first year but he decided to stay with it, and they just worked him into an early grave. He was too kind a man for those people, they just exploited his good nature.' She leaned into Alasdair, who put his arm around her.

'Thanks Soph. Anyway, how was your meeting tonight, any joy with a new figurehead for the show?'

She looked up at him excitedly. 'We did. Peter Finchburn came up with the very person and we all agreed, I'm going to pay a visit tomorrow to see if I can seal the deal as it were.'

'That's great news, well done! I'm sure it'll be all sorted tomorrow then – who is it you're going to ask?'

'We're going to ask Milton Scott.' She jumped as Alasdair leapt up from the sofa.

'What! You've got to be kidding?'

Chapter Fifteen

Emma's interview was at ten o'clock Wednesday morning but she was awake early and making breakfast by seven thirty. Abigail was working this morning so she was also up and having some All Bran. 'Are you ready for your big interview?' Emma sat down opposite her at the kitchen table with some toast.

'Ready as I'll ever be. I'm not sure what sort of things he'll ask me. Suppose I'll just need to wait and see; it should be fun I hope. How are you this morning? Have you spoken to Alasdair yet?' Abigail crunched her cereal without answering. 'You are going to speak to him today aren't you?'

'I'm not so sure you know. I was thinking about it last night and maybe he should come and apologise to me first.'

Emma tutted. 'Old people are always stubborn! Is it worth wasting any time over this? Life's too short.' She got up and started washing up the dishes and put the kettle on. 'Tea?'

Abigail got up and pushed her chair under the table. 'No thanks, I better get off to work,' then, smiling, 'I have a feeling someone might be phoning in sick today so I'll need to get a head start.'

Emma blushed slightly. 'Sorry, it does put you in a little bit of an awkward position. I'll make it up to you. What if I make us a nice dinner tonight? It'll be my way of saying thanks.'

'Ok, that would be lovely. I'll get some wine to go with it on my way home later.'

Emma sat down in the lounge with her cup of tea, trying to compose herself before her interview. She could feel her nerves starting to tingle and butterflies coming to life in her stomach. Calm down Emma, calm down, she thought looking about for something to distract her. She picked up yesterday's newspaper from the brass magazine rack and flopped it open. Her eyes scanned over the pages looking for nothing in particular when they stopped on one story which caught her attention.

> Jason Scott, 32, from Stirling, died yesterday in a house fire which ripped through his second-storey flat, and caused extensive damage to a neighbouring property. Mr Scott, who was unemployed and known to suffer from habitual drinking, is believed to have been intoxicated after leaving the Broadsword public house in the town and then accidentally started the fire on returning home. Fire Brigade spokesperson, Bill Menzies, commented that it appeared that Mr Scott had returned home and started to make a snack before falling asleep in his chair and had then been rendered unconscious from smoke inhalation. Mr Menzies added that they had found a square sausage in the toaster and concluded that Mr Scott had tried to cook the sausage in the toaster for a snack, however the fat dripping from it had been set alight by the heating element and the flames had spread to nearby curtains. No suspicious circumstances are being investigated . . .

She folded the paper up and put it aside as she got up. Set himself alight with a square sausage, she thought. Huh. And I think I've got problems!

As Emma was preparing herself for her interview, in the Mills household Sophie was cooking breakfast for Alasdair – he liked to have a full breakfast to keep him going all day. At least that was what he said, but in reality he liked a full breakfast to keep him going until lunch, via elevenses of course, which was a snack, but come lunchtime he would have a hearty meal to keep him going until dinner. Supper was another often forgotten meal these days he thought, a victim of healthy eating and not having food too close to bedtime. Bad enough, he thought, not being able to have cheese before bed without starving oneself altogether.

Alasdair came in and put his copy of *The Scotsman* on the table and sat down without a word. Sophie ignored him and kept poking the rashers of bacon around the frying pan and stirring the scrambled eggs, then dishing those with the beans, mushrooms, eggs and sausages. Alasdair kept reading the front of his paper as Sophie came over with the plates and stood opposite him. He folded his paper to the side and picked up his cutlery; however Sophie just stood there holding the plates expectantly. In the marital home it was the classic full English stand-off. Alasdair put his cutlery down again and looked up at Sophie, 'I'm still not going,' he said petulantly, 'I told you that last night and I'm not going to be swayed.' Sophie put the plates down in front of them both and sat down at the table, as Alasdair started tucking into his breakfast.

'I do recall you telling me that, however what I don't recall is getting any sort of explanation why you're against us having Milton Scott for our guest of honour. Not that it matters particularly since it's a committee decision, but given that you have shared interests it would be very helpful if you would help get him onboard.'

Alasdair spluttered as he choked on a piece of sausage. 'Look Sophie, Milton Scott and I definitely do not have anything shared, interests or otherwise. Yes, he may also be a collector but he's also been in trouble with the law. I don't understand why you would want an ex-convict to be associated with high tea?'

'He's not a convict,' she sighed, 'he was accused of some dodgy business deals but he was cleared so he's not got any criminal record. We checked. Besides, since he's been in Stirling he's become quite a local celebrity and is very generous to local charities and youth organisations. He's a successful businessman and local philanthropist now so I don't see how you could have any objection.' Alasdair said nothing and continued with his breakfast while Sophie eyed him tactfully. 'He's a descendent of Walter Scott you know, did you know that? I thought you'd enjoy meeting one of the Scott family since you're so keen on collecting all things to do with him. I believe Milton has some fantastic pieces in his collection. He might let you see them if you come with me.' Alasdair tried not to show any sign of weakening but Sophie had picked up on the momentary pause in his cutlery before he cut the next piece of sausage. Alasdair felt torn as Milton Scott did have some classic family heirlooms that were well known in collectors' circles and it would be wonderful to see them, but he just couldn't stand the man. He had to put his principles before everything else and he could not compromise them just for the chance to see some interesting artefacts or to help Sophie. That was that and he was adamant.

Chapter Sixteen

It took only ten minutes for Emma to walk into town and find herself standing outside The Pudding Furnace restaurant. The front window was covered in swirls of whitewash to block out any view of the interior, and pasted across the window was a sign saying 'One week to opening'. As she stood there a woman wearing a dark blue trouser-suit came out, an exasperated expression on her face, and marched off up the street muttering as she went. Emma watched her go, wishing she had dressed up a bit for her interview but since she didn't possess a suit of any description, her black jeans, blouse and a jumper would just have to do. She pushed open the door and a small bell chimed above as she walked in. 'We're not open yet!' a voice shouted through from what Emma presumed to be the kitchen.

She stepped forward a few paces into the restaurant. 'I'm here about the job. I called yesterday about an interview?'

A stocky, red-faced man appeared through the door and wiped his face with an old towel in his hand. 'Oh yes? And what magnificent ideas do you have to offer me? Self-stirring soup pans, waiters on roller skates? What was your name again?'

'Emma Harris. Is now a bad time or are you always like this?'

The man's expression softened slightly and he gestured her into a chair as he sat down opposite. 'Sorry, bad day. The way things are going here I'm not sure there's ever a good time.' Emma placed his accent as being from Glasgow but she couldn't quite picture him as a restaurant owner. 'I've just had a pipe in the kitchen spring a leak, the new oven isn't working and my drinks licence is tied up in red tape.'

Emma smiled sympathetically and pointed to the sign in the window. 'But at least you've still got a week until you open? You can get a lot done in a week I bet.'

'Oh the sign. Trouble is, I put that up last week before any of this happened so I'm already behind. Still, I like your positive attitude. Much like myself believe it or not.' He bellowed with laughter, 'Not that you'd think it eh? My name's Alec McAllister, proud owner of The Pudding Furnace.' He reached over and shook Emma's hand, before taking a small notebook out of his shirt pocket. 'So, you're here for the assistant manager's job? Do you have any experience?'

Emma flushed slightly. 'Not really, no, at least not running a restaurant. I work in the library at the moment but it's a bit quiet for me and I'd like something to get my teeth into. I think this would be just the thing.' Rather to her surprise he let out a mock cheer.

'Thank God for that. I've interviewed six people for this job so far and not one of them has come in looking like they were ready to do a day's hard graft. It's been all wine lists and rhubarb soufflés – not the thing at all for my place. What do you think of rhubarb soufflés?'

Emma shrugged. 'I've not tried one to be honest; it doesn't sound like it would beat a good sticky toffee pudding or ice cream.'

Alec laughed. 'Exactly. Why is it that everyone who wants to help manage my restaurant wants to try and turn it into the Ritz? You know I was in a restaurant the other day for lunch, research purposes and all that, and do you know what they had on the menu? Soup of the moment. Have you ever heard such a load of rubbish? I mean, soup of the moment! The waiter came to take our drinks order and told us what the soup was and when he came back with our drinks I asked him again what the soup was and he looked a bit puzzled. "You told me what it was a moment ago," I said, "but I assume it's changed since then?" Soup of the moment!'

Emma smiled. 'I've not really been to a lot of fancy restaurants to be honest Mr McAllister, but I'm a hard worker and I would be a great asset to your restaurant as I'm good with people too.'

'Then you might be just who I'm looking for as I'm not opening a fancy restaurant. I've always had a dream to open up someplace that people will want to visit all the time. The treat isn't coming to someplace fancy, it's about having comfort food. That's why it's called what it is, it's all about the puddings.'

'I think you're opening up at just the right time for a restaurant like this. I've been giving it a lot of thought,' Emma said enthusiastically, desperate to impress. 'The recession means people want comfort food and a place where the speciality is lovely puddings is just what people need to help make them feel better. I would definitely come here.' She looked around at the rustic décor and could see the attempt to create a nice, relaxing place. 'Especially with the fire going, it'll put people in a laidback mood.'

Alec leaned forward on the table. 'That's exactly what I think. Hard times mean people want something that will comfort them. It's like going back to your childhood when you always had nice things and you didn't have to think about the tough stuff. I want folk to come here to escape their troubles and not have to worry about fancy menus to get their heads around.'

Emma stifled a smirk. 'So no pudding of the moment on the menu then?' Alec laughed.

'You're not from Stirling are you?' she asked. 'How come you've opened up a restaurant here?'

'Am I not meant to be interviewing you?' Alec chuckled. 'I worked at the steelworks in Glasgow for years until they shut it down and that was that. Well, all those people looking for work there was nothing doing so I decided to retrain as a chef. It was always something I'd messed about with at home but it wasn't the sort of thing I could talk about with my mates or at work. I'd be slated for that with the guys I worked with before. But it turned out I had a knack for it and after paying my dues in some dives for a time I got a job in a nice restaurant in Glasgow. It was a nice place, but then it was bought over by a chain and they made it just the same as everywhere else and told me what I could cook. So I left.' He sat back. 'It would probably have been a good job but I just couldn't stand to do the same thing again, week after week, you know?'

Emma nodded. 'So that's when you came here?'

'No, I got a few other jobs but nothing seemed to keep me interested. I still had some of my payoff from my job tucked away so I decided to take a chance and start something up myself. And here I am, for better or worse.' He looked at her carefully, 'So, what's your story Emma?'

'I'll be honest Mr McAllister, I just need a chance and I can show you what I'm sure I could do.' She explained her background and recent saga, deciding that he might be the kind of man who just liked the honest approach.

He listened carefully, then replied, 'It does sound like you've had a bit of a rough time. Maybe you're worth taking a chance on. Like I say, sometimes people need a chance, I know that, and I like the idea of being master of my own place. How soon can you start?'

Chapter Seventeen

The Mercedes pulled up to the black wrought-iron gates and Sophie peered through the windscreen up the driveway to the large house beyond. The house had been an old manse and large mature trees and hedges gave it a grand look. One of the bushes on the left-hand side of the gates had been trimmed into the shape of a mouse, and on the opposite side one was trimmed into the shape of a man who had been made to look like he was holding a net. Next to the gates was an intercom at the level of the driver's window. Sophie waited. 'Well . . . ?'

Alasdair sighed loudly and lowered his window, 'I'm still not happy about this,' he said as he pressed the button.

'Yes, I think I got that but you're here now so you might as well behave with some measure of good grace about it. This means a lot to me and if we don't get Mr Scott on board then I'm going to have a bit of a hole in the event on Sunday as we haven't come up with any other worthwhile suggestions. Quick, answer the speaker . . .'

Alasdair leaned his head out of the window. 'It's Mr and Mrs Mills to see Milton Scott.'

A crackling voice came back through the intercom. 'Who? Do you have an appointment? Mr Scott is a very busy man and he can't be available to just anyone who happens to be passing.'

Alasdair turned to Sophie and rolled his eyes. 'Yes. We telephoned earlier and we have arranged to meet with him at twelve o'clock. It's a matter of great importance.' There was another crackling noise and then a creek as the gates started to swing open. Alasdair closed his window. 'Why is it that when you have to speak through an intercom it makes you feel like English isn't your first language? Ghastly contraptions.' They drove up to the house and parked outside the large, black, double front doors.

'Nice,' said Sophie.

'Awful,' Alasdair snorted. 'It's all for show. I bet he's put a stainless steel kitchen in there; it shouldn't be allowed in a period property.' Sophie didn't indulge him any further and got out of the car with Alasdair following,. 'If he's got a musical doorbell then I'm leaving now,' he said.

'Come on,' she rang the bell and a reassuring chiming noise came from within. 'There you go, no sign of "The Yellow Rose of Texas" to be heard.' A few moments later the door swung open and a young man with ruffled hair and a goatee beard stood before them.

'If you'd like to come in please,' he said, gesturing them in. They walked into a large hallway in which antique furniture was placed quite elegantly and a large grandfather clock ticked away at the bottom of the sweeping stairs. Sophie introduced herself to the young man.

'We're very pleased you could fit us in Mr Scott.'

He blushed. 'Oh, I'm not Mr Scott, I just work for him, he told me to let you in. I think he'll . . .'

'Thank you Graham,' a voice came from the stairs and Sophie and Alasdair looked up to see a man of around thirty in a dark pinstripe suit descending towards them. 'Mr and Mrs Mills, I'm sorry I couldn't greet you at the door but I was on a conference call to the States. Business never sleeps and all that.' He came over and shook their hands, giving them both a warm smile. 'That's the trouble with running an online business, we're always open somewhere and there's always someone asking a question. Still, it keeps the wolf from the door. Why don't we go into the drawing room and we can have some tea?' Sophie was smiling and glanced at Alasdair as Milton led them from the hallway into a large room.

'See, I told you he would be fine,' she whispered, 'he seems like a real gentleman, just who we need. Don't be difficult now, you know how you can go.'

Alasdair raised his eyebrows in surprise. 'Me?' he followed them into a large room which was again adorned with antique furniture and artwork around the walls. He was immediately drawn to a fine oak bookcase in which were housed an array of old books including, he noticed, a complete set of first edition *Waverly* novels by Sir Walter Scott.

'I thought those might catch your attention,' Milton Scott wandered over, 'very difficult to get a hold of but then you know that already I'm sure, not to mention how expensive they were. I managed to source them only recently and they're one of the most valued parts of my book collection.' Alasdair scanned along, looking at the other books on the shelf, all of which seemed to be first editions. *Kidnapped, Lady of the Lake, Ivanhoe* and a few others which made up quite a collection and, much to Alasdair's annoyance, stirred in him a pang of jealousy.

'Quite an impressive collection, I suppose. They must have cost you quite a bit of money. I'm surprised you could afford all of these given your recent proceedings, which were in the newspaper. I know from personal experience how legal costs can mount up.'

Sophie cast Alasdair a cold stare. 'Alasdair, you're not being very courteous to our host.'

Milton gestured casually but gave a curt smile. 'Oh, it was all in the papers so there's nothing to hide. I'm sure Mr Mills will also have read that I was completely cleared of all charges and even received an apology from HM Revenue and Customs for their preposterous hounding of me and my business.'

'I did read that, but then I don't always believe everything I read in the papers.'

'Hmm . . . perhaps only what you want to believe then I wonder? Speaking of which, I was very sorry to hear of your recent burglary. It must have been very traumatic for you Mrs Mills.'

Sophie, who was now sitting in a comfortable armchair, nodded agreeably. 'It was quite distressing, although they seem to have been after only one thing, so they thankfully didn't ransack our house and take any personal items. It was Alasdair that bore the fallout from it really. It must be quite worrying for you as well Mr Scott, knowing that something so valuable from your family heritage has been stolen?'

'Please, I think we can possibly work on first names now, can't we? I do get concerned when I hear about the careless loss of something valuable but thankfully those slippers weren't so important in the grand scheme of things.'

Alasdair could feel his hackles rising. 'It was not a careless loss as you put it. The police believe it may have been a professional gang that came in to steal them to order, for the very reason that they are so valuable. I suppose it's not such a big concern for you given that you're only very distantly descended from Walter Scott. If at all.'

Milton's mouth thinned but he didn't take the bait. 'We're all entitled to our opinion, Mr Mills, no matter how ill-informed. Now, if you'll excuse me for one minute I'll go and fetch us the tea and we can discuss the reason for your visit.' He left the room and Alasdair sat down in the chair next to Sophie, who was shooting death rays out of her eyes at him.

'What?' he asked innocently.

'What! Are you determined to ruin this for me? If you can't maintain at least a civil attitude then can I ask if you can just keep quiet?'

Alasdair sat back with his legs crossed. 'He was asking for it, Soph, lording it up over us like that. Careless loss indeed! But I realise you and the committee are intent on going ahead with this folly so I'll just keep out of it if that's what you want. I thought you brought me along so I could discuss our mutual interests. That's all I was doing.' He sat with an indignant look on his face, which did nothing to lessen Sophie's infuriation. She had thought he might be an asset but she should have known when it came to having to give ground to Milton Scott, Alasdair had put his line in the sand. Milton came back into the room with a tea tray, which he set down on the coffee table. A fine china teapot and cups were laid out along with a plate of cream cakes.

'I thought you might appreciate these, Sophie, given the impending event which I understand you are in charge of organising? Quite an undertaking, I hope it's all going well?'

Sophie sipped her tea. 'Oh well Mr Scott,' she paused, smiling, 'Milton. We're well on track and almost everything is in place. We have our performers, catering is in hand and the marquees are going up tomorrow. Even the weather forecast is looking quite favourable so it should be a good day. I'm afraid we just have one problem.'

'Oh?' He looked vaguely interested as Sophie explained about the Provost dropping out at the last minute due to family issues.

'You see Mr, I mean Milton, the guest of honour is a crucial part of our event. Rather like Stirling's position as a city in Scotland, the guest of honour will be the brooch that holds the entire thing together. So the reason we are here, as I'm sure an intelligent man like yourself must have guessed,' she could just see Alasdair silently tutting and rolling his eyes in her peripheral vision, 'is that we would be, well, honoured if you would accept the role as our guest of honour?'

Milton sat pondering for a moment. Inside he was relishing this and he would love nothing more than to accept. Despite being the most successful businessman in the area he had never been given the respect and recognition which he felt he deserved. It was he after all who gave generously to many local clubs and charities and he ran a highly successful online company from within Stirling, helping to maintain the city's acclaim as a centre for high-tech advances. His website www.itsworthwhat.com was a great success story, allowing people to upload pictures of their family heirlooms or collectibles and through his network of experts he could give them a value. There was no doubt that the biting recession had helped his business with ever increasing numbers of people searching their lofts for things to sell to bring them in some extra money which had meant a huge increase in business for Milton's website and therefore in his fortunes. To act as the guest of honour at such a big local event would go a long way to the city paying him back for all his good deeds. But one did have to play hard to get in these matters and if he agreed too easily it would not be such a coup – after all, for him to re-arrange his hectic schedule to fit them in would make it look much better. Sophie looked at him expectantly while Alasdair tried to eat a generously filled chocolate éclair without falling into the double jeopardy of both cream and chocolate smearing on his nose. Milton sprang to his feet and began pacing around the room, almost rending his garments in a show of great distress.

'Oh Mrs Mills, I would dearly love to help you out but my business and my commitments are great and I just can't think of a way out of them.'

Sophie looked disappointed. 'But Milton, the city is counting on you. This would not only help out our event but the city would owe you a huge debt of gratitude, even more than they do already.'

He paced around a little more for effect. 'Let me just go and check my diary and see if there's any way I can re-arrange my schedule.' He left the room and Sophie sat back feeling drained.

Alasdair leaned over. 'I think he might just go for it you know. If we can just offer him one of our kidneys then that might be enough to persuade him.'

She cast him a frosty glance. 'Very funny. I think he might accept, no thanks to you. She stopped as Milton came back into the room with his hands held up looking like an evangelical preacher.

'Good news! I can put back my conference call to New York and my meetings and I will be able to give you my time on Sunday.' Before Sophie could respond he continued, 'However, there is one thing I would ask in return. Just a small item.'

Sophie was on her feet and grinning inanely. 'Anything, what can we do?'

'I'd like the main stage to be named the Milton Scott Stage in honour of my being the guest at the inaugural event.'

Sophie glanced at Alasdair, who seemed disinterested. 'Well, I would have to run it by the committee but considering our position and your generous agreement I'm sure it will be fine.'

'Wonderful!'

Alasdair sighed and rose from his chair. 'Perhaps we should be going now and let Mr Scott get back to his computer games,' said Alasdair.

Sophie nodded and they were ushered towards the front door.

'So,' Milton said,' I assume you'll be in touch in the next couple of days to give me the details?' Sophie nodded again, barely able to speak with the huge relief she was feeling. 'I hope the police have some good news with your slippers too Alasdair. It's a shame when you have such a small collection to lose such a vital part of it.' Milton smiled at Alasdair, who for once decided to let it slide.

'I'm sure they will. Can I ask you one thing though?'

'Of course.'

'I was surprised when the slippers came up for auction that you weren't there bidding for them. In all seriousness, the fact that these were owned and worn by your illustrious ancestor, I would have thought you would have been desperate to get your hands on them?'

Milton paused a moment. 'No, not really. The problem is I have so many good-quality items that belonged to Walter, such as his writing set, and some manuscripts, that his old slippers weren't that much of a draw. Especially given the poor condition; I mean the hole in the sole of one of them is quite a disappointment. It really reduces their value, so much that I'm surprised they were sold at auction at all.'

Alasdair stared intently at him. 'The hole in the sole?'

'Yes, you should know, I think it was the left one wasn't it?'

Alasdair again kept staring. 'Yes, indeed it was,' he replied as Sophie placed a hand on his arm and gestured him out of the now open front door.

'Many thanks Mr Scott. Speak to you soon to go over timings.' The door was closed behind them and they got back into the car. 'What on earth was all that about?' Alasdair turned the key in the ignition and started down the driveway.

'It's just very interesting that he was able to tell me about the hole in the sole of one of the slippers.'

'Why? Everyone gets a chance to examine the lots before the auction don't they? He would have seen it then.' Alasdair pulled the car to a stop at the end of the driveway and glanced over at her.

'That would be true. Except the hole wasn't in them when they were auctioned; I did that when I tried them on at home to see if they would fit.'

Sophie looked confused. 'So how would Milton know about it then?'

'Good question,' he answered, as he steered the car onto the main road and headed for home.

Chapter Eighteen

Abigail left the library at two o'clock to walk the short distance home, unaware of the impending madness that would very shortly descend upon her in the form of one Alasdair Mills. The day was bright and sunny and, walking down the hill past the War Memorial, she could feel the heat on her face even through the trees. Since her fallout with Alasdair yesterday she had been feeling strangely subdued but also had a feeling of needing something to get her teeth into. The former was undoubtedly due to the disagreement with Alasdair, but the latter was a feeling of realising that something within her needed to be satisfied. Since Arthur had died she had been without any purpose or drive to move forward, but when she thought about it now she felt angry at wasting time when, as Emma had said, life is too short. Abigail could remember back to when her mother died and her father had gone for months without taking care in his appearance, even leaving the house without shaving, which was something he would never have done, or been allowed to do for that matter. Then one day he appeared dressed as he used to be, cleanly shaven and with his favourite tie carefully knotted under the collar of an immaculately ironed shirt.

'It just occurred to me,' he had told the younger Abigail, 'what would your mother say about all this?' That was it. He seemed to have come to the realisation that life did have to go on, even though it was sometimes the hardest thing to do, but the main part of his grieving had passed. Abigail felt that she would have come to that point, but to have someone make it clear just how she had changed had brought her to a sudden realisation. What would Arthur say about all this?

As she approached her front path she could see on the doorstep a familiar ginger-coloured article. 'Hello Waffles,' she said cheerfully, 'it's nice to see you again. Are you coming in for some milk?' As she opened the front door Waffles padded in and made his way through to the kitchen, having a sniff as he went. Emma was already in the kitchen, various cookbooks and cooking utensils, bowls and ingredients spread over the worktop. Abigail surveyed the scene.

'Goodness, you're hard at work! This looks like it's going to be a sumptuous meal tonight.'

Emma handed her a saucer for Waffles' milk. 'Well, you can't have a meal with the new assistant manager of The Pudding Furnace and it not be a treat!'

'You got the job?'

'I got the job!' Emma was beaming. 'I just need to confirm my start date as soon as possible. I spoke to the council and they say that since I was on work experience and I've got a job, I can leave as soon as I want but to clear it with the library manager. Do you think there'll be any problem leaving straightaway?'

Abigail looked doubtful. 'Oh, I can't see that being allowed Emma. You would normally need to give a month's notice at least.'

Emma's face fell. 'Really?'

'No!' Abigail laughed, 'I shouldn't think it'll be a problem at all – we're not short-staffed really. I'll put in a word for you and we'll sort it out. That's great news though, a new beginning for you. What was the place like?' Emma gave Abigail the story of the interview and the plans for the restaurant, only being interrupted by an incessant miaowing coming through from the front door as Waffles demanded to be let back outside. Abigail wandered through and opened the door as the cat took a curious look around before walking out and over the gardens to start miaowing at a house a few doors up. Abigail watched him go. 'Cats!' she thought, 'they'll never be stuck.' She was about to close the door when she caught sight of a familiar figure lurking on the pavement just outside her garden.

Alasdair showed himself at the garden gate. 'Hello Abigail, how's things?'

Abigail was glad to see him but her stubborn streak wouldn't let her admit it. 'Fine, and you?'

Alasdair winced. 'Well, bit of a development really about my burglary. I've spoken to Sophie about it but I wanted to speak to you too if possible?' Abigail couldn't help wondering what it was that would make Alasdair, whose stubborn streak was also rather well developed, come around and break the albeit brief silence between them.

Abigail gestured to him. 'I think you had better come in, or else someone will call the police with the way you're loitering about there.'

Emma was in the middle of stirring a sauce on the cooker when Abigail came in with Alasdair, 'Emma, this is Alasdair Mills. Alasdair this is Emma Harris, my house guest.' Alasdair held out his hand and Emma shook it.

'So, you work at the library with Abby don't you?'

Emma shook her head. 'Not any more, I just got a new job today. I'm making a meal for Abigail and I to celebrate. I take it you two have made up now then?' There was an awkward silence as neither Abigail nor Alasdair were prepared to admit that they had made up since each of them was expecting the other to apologise first. Emma threw up her hands, sighing loudly, 'For goodness sake, you're like two bairns. Alasdair, Abigail is sorry she yelled at you and lost her temper.' Abigail was about to protest but Emma kept talking to cut her off. 'She knows you had her best interests at heart and what's more she thinks you were right.'

Alasdair's expression grew smug at being vindicated but Emma wasn't going to let him get away with it either. 'Alasdair, since I've just met you I can't apologise to Abigail for you, but I can only hope that it will be the next thing you say. From what I understand you were condescending and pompous towards Abigail and, yes, she may need to get her mojo back but she needs the support of her friends rather than them trying to manoeuvre her around.' She stood with her arms folded, looking at Alasdair, then at Abigail, then back at Alasdair again. 'Well?'

They both glanced at each other and, as expected, it was Abigail who took the higher ground. 'I'm sorry I was angry with you Alasdair, I do appreciate that you were only trying, in your usual incomprehensible way, to look after my best interests. I shouldn't have said what I did about you and Arthur either, that was unforgivable.'

Alasdair smiled. 'I can't deny I was a bit hurt by that Abby, but in the spirit of harmony, I apologise for handling things the wrong way. I just wanted to see the old Abigail back again. Probably best next time that I get Sophie to have a word with you if there's anything we're worried about. I'll never profess to understand the female mind.' He looked at Emma, 'It looks as if you'll be quite the guardian angel for Abby?'

Emma smiled towards Abigail. 'I will, so you'll need to be on your best behaviour. It's the least I can do for her after what she's done for me. Now, I have too much to do in here for you two to be in here as well. Sorry Abigail, I know it's your kitchen but if you wouldn't mind going into the lounge to chat then I'll bring in the tea?'

Abigail chuckled again. 'You're the boss it would seem at the moment. Come on then Alasdair let's hear the latest with your burglary.' She walked out of the kitchen and Alasdair followed, although a moment later he popped his head back around the door.

'By the way Emma, no milk or sugar for me – I like my tea the way God intended.' He turned to leave and then paused, looking back at her, 'And what the blazes is a mojo?'

Chapter Nineteen

Abigail took her usual armchair next to the fire and facing the bay window, while Alasdair sat down on the sofa facing the fireplace. He looked around the room as he was vaguely aware something was different but couldn't quite put his finger on it rightaway, then it struck him, 'You've put away all the old photograph albums from the sideboard Abby. I thought it looked tidier than usual, have you done with looking through them?'

Abigail looked out of the window. 'Sort of, although it's more a case of being done with wallowing in the past. I know where they are if I want them. I think it's maybe time to look forward and see what's still to come down the road.'

'Quite right Abby,' he said, 'and speaking of that, I think I may have stumbled onto something quite interesting.'

'Really?' she said, suddenly intrigued. 'Do tell?'

Emma came through the door with the tea tray and Alasdair waited rather impatiently while she poured both he and Abigail a cup, passing out the chocolate biscuits as well to which he helped himself to three. Once she was back in the kitchen he seemed lost for a moment enjoying his biscuits, given that Sophie had tried to limit the biscuits kept at his house to trim his waist. 'Well? Are you going to spill the beans or not?' Abigail asked.

'It's one of life's simple pleasures Abigail, to savour a nice chocolate biscuit with your tea.' She raised her eyebrows expectantly.

'Anyway,' he said, 'I think I may have a good idea who was behind the theft of my slippers.'

He relayed to Abigail the story of his visit to Milton Scott with Sophie earlier that day and, in no uncertain terms, how the man had tried to lord it over him as if he were royalty. Abigail listened carefully, taking in the details. 'But what exactly makes you think he stole them? Maybe he found out about the hole in them some other way, maybe by something in the papers?'

Alasdair shook his head. 'Impossible. I didn't tell anyone about it as I was more than a little embarrassed to have damaged them. I mean after paying that amount of money for them and then putting a hole in them.' He looked a tiny bit sheepish as Abigail just laughed.

'I knew fine well you wouldn't be able to resist trying them on. Did they fit?'

'No, too small, hence the hole. But the point is that how did he know about the hole if he hasn't seen them since they were stolen?'

Abigail laid her head back on the chair. 'It's a strange one, but I find it hard to believe he would go to the trouble of stealing them. I mean he's got such a collection of stuff already that he wouldn't miss those tatty old things.'

'Abby, Abby, Abby,' Alasdair took up his position in front of the fire, which was where he usually felt he could lecture from most effectively, 'you're not thinking like a collector, let alone one where there's a long family connection like Milton Scott has. He does have a good collection of pieces but his collection isn't complete, and if I was to hold onto the slippers then it never would be. A collector's driving ambition is to complete their collection. To have a collection which can't be completed is bad enough for any of us but when money isn't the problem it must grate on his nerves something terrible knowing that I hold that power over him and his ambition.' He raised himself up on his toes and loomed towards her for emphasis. 'That kind of feeling can make a man do anything.' Having finished his point he strolled over and looked out of the bay window, as was also customary, while he allowed some time for the recipient of his lecture to take in his words of wisdom. He knew that in due course there would be a further questioning of his logic and from his position at the window he felt most at ease, being able to spin Columbo-like around and knock it for six. Abigail was well accustomed to this pattern but was prepared to indulge him yet again.

'Maybe he was offered them from a, what are they called? A fence? He might not have stolen them at all.'

Alasdair spun around, raising a hand in the air. 'Yes, but if that was the case why didn't he go to the police and tell them about it. Even if that was the case, Abby, it still shows he has something to be held accountable for – handling stolen goods if nothing else!'

'So I assume you've gone to the police and told them what you know?'

He sat down again on the couch. 'I phoned them this afternoon and spoke to the sergeant who's looking after my case. They said it wasn't enough to go on to get a search warrant and they certainly weren't going to start accusing a high-profile local figure on the basis of my suspicions. He didn't say as much but I get the feeling the police know that Milton Scott and I don't get along.'

Abigail folded her arms. 'There you go then.'

Alasdair shook his head. 'No, I'm telling you there's something fishy about all this. I can't stand the thought that he might have my slippers and be laughing behind my back. It was bad enough today with his 'Ooh look, here's a set of first edition *Waverly* novels I've just acquired.' He was just trying to rub my nose in it.'

Emma appeared at the door, 'Abigail, sorry to disturb you but I'm a little ahead of schedule. Are you ready for dinner now?'

Abigail nodded. 'Lovely. I'll just show Alasdair out and I'll be with you.'

Alasdair looked over towards the kitchen door. 'Something smells nice,' he said, 'I'm in no rush you know?'

'Come on Alasdair,' Abigail gestured him towards the door, 'you've already had more biscuits than you're supposed to and we're not feeding you here so that you can go home and get fed there too. I know your game.' She bundled him towards the door. 'And don't start obsessing about Milton Scott and your half-baked theory. I'd be pretty certain that he's got more important things to worry about than your slippers.'

Alasdair looked doubtful, but just shrugged and then headed out for home.

Emma was setting the table when Abigail came back in.

'Just putting the finishing touches to the table Abigail, everything's ready.'

Chapter Twenty

Next morning, Sophie was bustling around the lounge when Alasdair came down for breakfast. He looked around the mess of papers and folders littering the furniture. 'You were up early this morning Soph, what's the panic?'

'What do you mean what's the panic? It's only three days to go and we've got a lot to do. According to my plan of attack, Thursday we've got the stage and the marquees going up and then we need to get tables and chairs set up. I take it you'll be able to lend a hand?'

He feigned surprise. 'Me? Surely the committee don't want me, a simple layman, to be involved with the big event? I didn't think my input was appreciated.'

Sophie gave him one of her withering looks. 'Grow up Alasdair. You know very well it's all hands on deck now. I told the committee last night we could count on your help as well today since you wouldn't want to let me down.' She walked over and put her arms around him, 'You wouldn't want to let me down now would you?'

He smiled. 'No, you know fine I wouldn't.' She kissed him quickly and then started beavering around the various folders on the coffee table.

'Right, if you can meet me at the park at twelve that will let me get the marquee people organised and you can help with the lifting and carrying. We're a bit short of strong able-bodied men to help us get the chairs and things in place.'

Alasdair smiled at her. 'I said I would help, you don't need to lay it on quite so thick.'

Sophie laughed. 'Good. Just wanted to make sure. I'm off now to meet up with some of the committee for a project update. See you later.' She kissed him again as she flew out of the door with a pile of papers and folders under one arm and her coat flapping about under the other.

After a breakfast of grapefruit and orange juice which Sophie had laid out for him, and two kippers smeared with garlic butter which Alasdair had secreted at the back of the fridge for himself, he wandered through to his study with the post and opened up a large brown envelope, pulling out a sheaf of leaflets. His attempts at becoming more green hadn't exactly been powering ahead, although he had tried to be less wasteful, but the information he held in his hands would hopefully be a big help, and with relatively little pain for him to bear. He was just reading over them when the phone rang. He looked over at the clock, only nine thirty, very early for anyone to call he thought, picking up the receiver. 'Hello?'

'Alasdair?' It was Abigail's voice. 'I think you had better come and see this. I'm at work if you're free.' Alasdair's curiosity was piqued since Abigail had never made such a call in all their years of knowing one another.

'Abby? Yes, I've nothing on this morning until I meet Sophie later. I'll pop round shortly.' He hung up the phone, glad to have an excuse to get out of the house, and headed out the door to the library.

As he arrived, he could see Abigail watching for him from a window and she met him in the entrance foyer. 'Hello Abby. What's up?'

She put a finger to her lips. 'Shh, not so loud. I've got something to show you in here.' She led him through to the lending library and around the desk, where a pile of newspapers were stacked on the counter. A few people browsed around the shelves of books and if any of them were to be watching, of which none of them were, they would think that some great conspiracy was being hatched with the low timbre of Abigail's voice (the truth being that if you work in the place long enough then hushed becomes your normal speaking volume). She picked up a paper from the pile and laid it on the counter in front of them. 'I was going through these newspapers from last week which we had to archive for the reference library upstairs and since we're quiet I was just having a quick flick through some of them, you know to catch up on any news.' She glanced at Alasdair, who looked blankly at the paper.

'I don't get it Abby, what's so special about this one?'

'Look!' she rifled through the pages and then laid it down again. 'It's probably nothing but I thought it was quite a coincidence with what you said yesterday.' Alasdair glanced over the page at the story Abigail was talking about.

Nineteenth Century first edition books stolen

A collection of unique books by Sir Walter Scott were stolen from a farmhouse near Elgin earlier this week. The items, a set of twenty-four 'Waverly' 1842 edition books were reported missing from a private collection after a burglary at the house. Police have no leads at the moment but their enquiries are continuing. Grampian Police are investigating the incident which is believed to have happened between 7.30 p.m. and 9.00 p.m. last Wednesday. A spokesman commented, 'The items stolen are very rare and valuable and I would ask the public that if they are offered these books for sale to contact police as soon as possible.'

Alasdair's mouth fell open as he read the article again. 'I don't believe it,' he said. 'He's got his crooked scheme going all over the country! It must be him, he told me he had just acquired a set of these books. Just acquired – and look at this!' Abigail ushered him out into the foyer again as people were starting to look over.

'Now you don't know that. You can't tell me that the set of books that Milton Scott has are the same as these ones. There must be a good few sets of these first editions around I expect.'

Alasdair was shaking his head. 'No, I think we're onto something. The trouble is I doubt if the police will believe me, I mean it's not exactly evidence is it?' He paced around, clearly agitated by this new piece of information.

'Alasdair,' Abigail said, 'I have to get back to work. Perhaps we can discuss this later?' He didn't seem to hear. 'Alasdair?'

He stopped suddenly. 'Sorry Abby, I need to go. You should get back to work too. Talk later.' He rushed out of the door and into the street, turning right towards the town.

Chapter Twenty-One

Alasdair walked through the town, going nowhere in particular but his mind buzzing with the possibility that Milton Scott had been behind not only his burglary but others into the bargain. He walked down past the Burgh, and then into the Marches just to have somewhere to walk around and try to think. At the last of the shops he turned around to go back again and as he did so, found himself outside the bookshop. 'Where do you learn anything if not from a teacher?' he thought, as he went into the bookshop. It was after only a few minutes of browsing that he found the very thing, and took it down from the shelf to buy it immediately.

Sophie was standing next to the Victorian drinking fountain in the King's Park, holding a clipboard and counting up the chairs which stood in stacks along the tarmac road leading to the large grassy area on which the marquees now stood. She saw Alasdair hurrying through the gate towards her. 'Sorry I'm a little late, got held up in town. You'll never believe . . .'

She cut him off mid-sentence. 'Yes, I'm sure you've got a good excuse, as always! But I've got a bit of a problem here and I need you to start lifting chairs into the marquees and setting them up at the tables. The tent people were late which meant the marquees weren't up by the time the chairs were delivered; the chair people couldn't wait for the tent people. I really could do without this.'

Alasdair looked at the huge pile of chairs. 'I can't lift all of these by myself.'

'I'm not asking you to lift them all by yourself. But maybe you could make a start since those of us that have been here for the last hour are rather exhausted having carried the tables into the tents.'

'Ah, OK.' He picked up a small pile of chairs and carried them off into the furthest-away marquee, grumbling as he did so. 'This isn't going to help my back you know,' he shouted over his shoulder, but Sophie was too busy to hear. The next three hours were spent lifting, carrying and positioning chairs around the tables in the large tents. Standing back once it was all done, Alasdair had to admit that the set-up was rather good, and once the finishing touches and decorations were put up tomorrow it would look even better.

Sophie smiled at him. 'Thank you for helping, it's been an all hands on deck sort of day today. Are you OK?' Alasdair had been sitting down and on trying to stand when Sophie came over, he couldn't quite get himself completely vertical.

'I think my back has gone, I can't stand up straight.'

Sophie rubbed his lower back vigorously. 'Poor thing, you've worked really hard. Let's get you home and into a hot bath and then some of your old dad's homemade liniment should sort you out.'

Abigail was placing books back into the shelves, wondering why it was that browsers couldn't put a book back into the same space in which they found it. It's not rocket science, she thought as she shuffled books around, if you can read you must have at least some grasp of the alphabet. Valerie Stewart, Abigail's colleague, sidled up beside her, 'You've got a phone call. I think it's that man who was in here earlier, a Mr Mills? He did say he was sorry to bother you but it's urgent and he knows you don't really have anything to do in a library that can't wait.'

'That sounds like Alasdair,' Abigail said as she went over to the desk to pick up the phone. 'Hello?' A loud voice echoed down the receiver.

'Abby! I think I've had an epiphany! Can you meet me later to help with something?'

'What sort of thing? Where are you anyway, there's a bad echo?'

'I'm lying on the bathroom floor, my back's gone again. Sophie rubbed some of the family liniment into it and I wanted to lie on a hard surface to see if it would help. Well, plus Sophie won't let me into the rest of the house with this stuff on because she says it'll strip the wallpaper.' Abigail knew exactly what Sophie meant. The Mills family liniment was a foul-smelling concoction which had been passed down the generations in Alasdair's family. Reputedly a mixture first used by great-great-grandfather Mills in the Boer War, it contained no less than nine ingredients, which were difficult to identify but all highly odourous. Abigail had been given a small coloured bottle of it once when she hurt her back gardening, and after applying it had gone for a lie down on her bed to let it work its magic. To be fair to the stuff, it had helped her back, but it had also taken the colour out of the bedspread, leaving an imprint of her body as if it were the Turin Shroud. Abigail had asked then what on earth was in it but Alasdair said he was sworn to secrecy and, in fact, the Coca-Cola company had once contacted his grandfather to ask his advice on how to keep a recipe secret.

Abigail sat down at the desk. 'What is it you want me to help you with?'

'Well, I've been doing some research after a trip to the bookshop and I have a plan. But I need your help to pull it off. Let me explain ...'

Chapter Twenty-Two

Emma walked into the kitchen of The Pudding Furnace to find her new boss, Alec McAllister, with his head in the oven. 'Hi Alec, are things that bad?' He pulled his head out and sat on the floor, looking at her.

'Ha ha, if only you were as good an electrician as a comedian. Then again . . .' he gave a wry smile as he looked back around and into the oven. 'It seems to be something to do with the fan; it's not moving at all when the oven's on.'

'Why don't you call the company who supplied it to you. You must have some sort of warranty with it, don't you?'

'I've already called them but they can't come until tomorrow. I thought I might be able to fix it before then, but looks like I can't. I should have gone for a barbecue restaurant, that would have been easier.' He hauled himself up and threw the spanner he was holding into a toolbox. 'So, ready for some work?'

She nodded. 'I am, I'm keen to get started. What do we have to do today?' Alec pulled a sheet of paper from his pocket and unfolded it and showed her the list of things to be done.

'Take your pick from any one of these and make a start. Just give me a shout if you need any help.' Emma scanned the list and decided it would be good to go for something important first to show she could do the job, and with that she went through to the restaurant and sat down with the laptop to try to design the menu layout. The dishes on the menu looked wonderful and as she was setting them down, choosing fonts, and laying them out on the page, she found she was enjoying herself. Apart from the occasional clanging from the kitchen, usually followed by a yell of some description, she had a most pleasant afternoon.

At around five o'clock Alec came through from the kitchen and looked over her shoulder. 'That's pretty good,' he said, 'if we've got an oven to cook those dishes then we're definitely in business.'

'It'll be fine. I'm finding that even when things look bleak you find that they can work out quite well.'

Alec sat down at the next table. 'It's good to have someone else here to talk to about things, makes it a bit easier. I hadn't realised what a big job this was going to be – I should have hired someone sooner to help me. So what is it that you've found so bad and it's worked out?' Emma looked a bit uneasy at the question and Alec backtracked. 'Sorry, none of my business. I'm used to knowing quite a lot about the people I work with. There were few secrets in the steelworks, or in the kitchens either come to that. The goings on some people get up to would make you cringe at times.'

Emma nodded. 'Tell me about it.' She pointed to the screen. 'I've finished this so I can start on something else.'

Alec shook his head. 'Nah, that'll do us for today. I'm taking an awfy scunnering to this now. I could do with a break. You get off home and we'll make a start again tomorrow.' Emma got her coat on and let herself out as Alec was switching off the lights.

'OK, see you tomorrow Alec.'

'Aye, see you.'

As they both went their separate ways from the restaurant, further down the hill Emma's now estranged husband, John, watched with anger as she disappeared out of sight.

Chapter Twenty-Three

Abigail occasionally pondered on her friendship with Alasdair and, particularly at times like this, she couldn't quite figure it out. Yes, Alasdair and her husband had been business partners and had played the odd round of golf, but it was really since Arthur had died that Alasdair had made a bigger effort to get to know her. There was nothing improper about the whole thing, goodness knows they were both too old and too settled for that sort of thing and Alasdair was devoted to Sophie. But she thought, at heart, it might be that Alasdair had seen something in her that he thought she was as eccentric as him and it had meant a new colleague to bounce his mad ideas off. Abigail would normally have dismissed such a thought, since she would argue the point if anyone had told her they thought she was an eccentric, but at this precise moment it would have been a tough argument to win.

Abigail was parked outside Alasdair's house, the engine of the mobile library van idling over loudly as she watched for the front door to open and Alasdair to appear, which he duly did. His face lit up as he saw her and he waved excitedly. 'Abby, you're a star!' He raced down the front path and opened the passenger door. 'I wasn't sure if you'd be able to get it but it looks exactly the part.' He climbed in and saw Abigail glowering at him. 'What's up?'

'What's up? I must have gone mad to agree to this. Explain to me again how this is going to work?' Alasdair closed the door and pulled his seatbelt across.

'It's quite simple, Abby, we're on a surveillance mission. I was out walking this afternoon and wandered into the bookshop in town and all of a sudden it became clear.' He pulled a book out of the backpack he was carrying and handed it to Abigail.

She looked at the book and then back at Alasdair. '*The Private Detective's Handbook* – you're not serious are you?'

Alisdair smiled broadly. 'It makes perfect sense. The police aren't giving this the attention it deserves and they probably don't have the manpower to dedicate to solving it, so we're going to take up the challenge! I don't know why I didn't think of this rightaway; we could crack this and put the perp behind bars quite quickly I feel.'

Abigail raised her eyebrows. 'The perp?'

Alasdair pointed to the book. 'There's a glossary at the back of the book; I've been brushing up on my detecting parlance.'

Abigail gave the book a quick flick and then looked back at him. 'I assume therefore that this is the reason for your outfit too?' Alasdair was dressed in black trousers, a black shirt and a brown overcoat with the collar turned up. A wide-brimmed hat completed the ensemble. One thing was certain; when he took up an interest he embraced it wholly and without hesitation.

'I paid a quick visit to McAree's this afternoon too, no one has a better selection of hats in the city and I got this coat there as well. If we're going to be detectives then we need to look the part.' He reached into his bag again. 'I got you these sunglasses and a Paisley headscarf so you can be disguised as well.'

He handed them to her and she turned them over in her hands. 'It's going to be dark soon. How am I supposed to carry out surveillance when I can't see anything? And as for this scarf . . . well.'

'OK then don't wear them, but don't come running to me when you've been made.'

Abigail's eyebrow raised again. 'When I've been made?'

'Page 142, in the glossary. I would suggest you keep the book and look it up so you don't stand out like a sore thumb!' He very deliberately pulled up the collar of his coat, 'Shall we go?' Abigail shook her head as she drove the library van down the road and turned left at the bottom.

After driving the long way around, they pulled up and parked just over and a little up the road from Milton Scott's house. Alasdair slouched down into the passenger seat stretching his legs out into the footwell. 'Isn't this exciting Abby? I can't believe we're actually on a stake-out now.' Abigail sat upright in the driver's seat, her legs cramped behind the pedals.

'I can't believe it either – so this is us being incognito is it?'

'Indeed it is. Who's going to suspect the mobile library van?'

'Oh yes,' Abigail replied, 'I mean a twenty-foot-long van sat in the street is just the kind of thing that makes us invisible. What are we looking for exactly anyway?'

Alasdair shrugged. 'Not sure yet but I have a feeling we'll know it when we see it.' He picked up his backpack from the storage area behind his seat and rifled through it. 'I've got some supplies to keep us going. Here we are.' Abigail watched as he placed on the dashboard a red thermos flask containing hot tea, two blue plastic mugs, a box containing some sandwiches and two of what looked to be fudge doughnuts.

'What's in the sandwiches?' she asked.

'Corned beef. I wanted to try and keep it quite authentic and I think the old private eyes would have liked a bit of corned beef.'

'I always thought they would have bagels or something like that, and coffee? I think we have a very British stake-out menu here.' She glanced over to the big house opposite, 'He's got a nice house. There's obviously money in the internet.'

Alasdair puffed out his cheeks. 'Money in crime more like it, he's probably got my slippers and stripped them down and sold them for parts.'

'Who's he going to have sold them to?' she asked, 'Timpson's? I would think he'll have better things to do, if he had anything to do with it in the first place! This seems daft wasting our time with this.' She glanced at Alasdair who was just staring intently at the house, 'Still we're here now so we might as well see what we can . . .' She stopped suddenly as there was a loud knock at the main door in the back of the van where the library section was located. They looked at each other, startled for a moment, before Abigail motioned Alasdair through the door behind the seats and they crept quietly passed the bookshelves towards the sound of the knocking.

'Hello? Anyone in there?' An elderly woman's voice drifted through the closed door.

'What do we do now Abby?' Alasdair whispered. 'Should we pretend not to be in?'

'She's probably heard us moving around already or maybe talking at the front. Let me deal with it and I'll see what she wants.' Alasdair slinked back behind a bookshelf as Abigail walked over and pushed open the door to see a grey-haired woman smiling back at her. 'Can I help you?' Before Abigail could stop her the woman smiled and clambered up the two small steps into the van.

'Well, yes. I missed you when you were round earlier you see so when I noticed you were back again I thought I would come and get some books out. It's not usual that you come round again in the evening is it? I thought it was a bit odd.' Abigail flashed a quick glance towards Alasdair who held out his palms, his face slightly panicked, before turning back to the old woman.

'Erm . . . it's a new service we're providing – for speed readers.' The woman looked confused. 'Yes, we've had reports of speed readers in the area and, well, you know those people, they can read a book in a couple of hours so imagine how many they can get through in a day! Working in the council, we need to cater for everyone you know so here we are again' Remarkably, the old woman seemed to be buying into this.

'I suppose you do, I never gave it a thought. But then you have large print books for those with bad sight and the books on tape too so why not do something for these, speed readers is it? It's such an inclusive world we live in now isn't it?'

Abigail nodded. 'Yes. So we better clear the library area here –
they come in at quite a pace to browse as well you know. We have
to secure the books into the shelves.'

The woman looked startled. 'Really? I thought that was to stop
them falling out when you're driving the van around?'

'Oh, lots of people think that but we know the real reason
now don't we? Now, off you go before you get caught in the
whirlwind.' Abigail cajoled the woman back out of the door and
down onto the street. 'Thanks for coming and we'll be back at
our usual time next week.' She closed the door and then flopped
into a moulded plastic chair. Alasdair came out from behind the
shelves, laughing and clapping his hands.

'Well done Abby! I've never heard such a lot of nonsense but
that was quick thinking – you're definitely cut out for this game,
coming up with a cover story like that.' Abigail just looked up
at him, nothing more to say for the moment, but feeling quite
exhilarated by what she had just done. There might be some life
in this old dog yet. Alasdair was climbing back in to the front cab.

'Come on Abby, you deserve a sandwich for that!'

Chapter Twenty-Four

The corned beef sandwiches slowly dwindled as the evening wore on into early morning. They chatted back and forth on a variety of subjects; families, the economy, the fact that common sense was being evolved out of the species. A fact which they noted was particularly prevalent where padding had been placed around lamp posts to stop people who were using their mobile phones from hurting themselves when they walked into them. Thankfully these pockets of common senseless were few and far between and certainly had not infiltrated Stirling so far. Perhaps having a university of some note was helpful with this they thought.

They watched the windows and doors, gardens and grounds of Milton Scott's house but nothing seemed to stir. A few of the windows had blinked into darkness, like eyes closing, as the night had passed but a few lights still remained. 'I wonder how much energy they use in that house,' Alasdair said thoughtfully. 'I bet they could use a bit of my Green Light philosophy, maybe even to go the whole hog and get a wind turbine, something like that.'

'They might already be doing things like that – you tend to find people in his position want to be seen to be taking the lead. Anyway, how's your green movement going – embraced all of the things on your list yet?' He hesitated, although a faint flicker of a smile crept over his mouth.

'I'm not so sure that I need to go too mad with all that stuff you know. I can offset a huge part of my carbon footprint in one fell swoop and it will hardly cost me anything at all to do it, and certainly it won't mean giving up my trips abroad.'

Abigail sighed. 'I thought you'd given up all this offsetting nonsense, isn't this just like the light-bulbs again?' He shook his head vigorously.

'Absolutely not. Abby, this is a stroke of genius which has to be seen to be believed. Clearly you need to have vision but thankfully I'm more than blessed there and I was delighted to see that the boffins had come up with a solution.' He slowly, but not without a little flourish, produced an A4 size pamphlet from his backpack and laid it on the steering wheel in front of Abigail. Abigail leaned over and read the title, 'Eco Cemeteries', and then underneath was the tagline, 'Saving the world from the beyond'. Abigail sat back in her seat and just stared at him.

'Oh my God, what on earth is this?'

Alasdair was clearly thrilled. 'It's genius, Abby. This company is set up for people just like me who want to offset their carbon emissions. What they have is a cemetery and each grave is linked up to a collection chamber. When you're buried, the coffin is linked up by a pipe and as your body decays naturally, the gases which are emitted are collected and then burned off to create power. It's incredible! It means that you don't have to worry about your carbon footprint while you're alive as it's all offset after you've gone. What do you think?' He sat back waiting for the admiration to begin, and was somewhat surprised when it didn't materialise.

'Well, I think that's fabulous Alasdair. I mean why don't we just all do that, we can do whatever we like while we're alive and then let it all be made right when we've gone.'

He looked taken aback. 'But . . . I don't think you understand.'

'Oh, I understand alright. This is designed for people who want to go through life without a thought for the environment or future generations. This is just typical of the world today – we want to be responsible but no one is willing to make the sacrifices necessary. It's shocking and I can't believe you're considering that this is a good idea! What would be a great idea is if everyone played their part now and then this could be an added bonus later.'

Alasdair looked a little unsure, as Abigail flicked through the brochure. 'Not to mention the fact that it says in the small print here that it would take around a hundred people to compensate for one short flight between Edinburgh and London. Look, just under where they tell you the price is eight thousand pounds to do this.' Alasdair looked intently at their surveillance target trying to ride this out, but Abigail continued. 'And have you seen this bit?' She held open the pamphlet on a page with diagrams of how it all worked; a small black-line diagram in which curly lines seemed to be flowing up a chimney which in turn was linked to a turbine generating power, and further down the line a family happily cooking their dinner on a cooker running from the energy provided. Alasdair took the brochure and looked down at it.

'Hadn't really looked at it that closely,' he admitted. 'You might be right but I'm not going to rule it out just yet.' He stuffed the pamphlet into his backpack for future consideration as Abigail gazed out of the side window.

'Oh, Alasdair. There isn't a quick fix with these things you know, you just have to put the work in.'

'Look Abigail . . .'

She turned towards him. 'You can't defend this Alasdair.'

He pointed towards the large house. 'No, look!' Abigail stared out towards the road where Alasdair was pointing and saw the small white van coming towards them, its indicator blinking to show it was turning into Milton Scott's driveway.

'Oh my God, Castle Roofing! It's them. I have to say I'm quite impressed that even the criminal fraternity think to indicate; you would have thought they wouldn't bother. It's OK to burgle a house but don't forget your highway code!'

'I knew he was involved in this, I knew it. I told you and Sophie but no one would believe me. They look like they're going around the back – we should call the police!' He reached for his phone but Abigail clamped her hand over his, trapping it in his pocket.

'What exactly would we tell them? Apart from anything else I could lose my job for taking the library van without permission and I'm sure it won't go down well that we're carrying out unauthorised surveillance on someone's house. We'll probably be arrested for loitering and car theft!'

Alasdair wasn't to be swayed. 'We need to do something Abby, this could be something big.'

'It might be but here's another thought – what if they're actually going to his house to burgle it now? With his valuable collection he'd be a prime target.'

Alasdair bit his lip. 'Bloody hell Abby, you could be right. We need to do something though, we can't just sit here, otherwise we might as well have stayed at home.' Abigail reached over into the glovebox, rifling through the contents and producing a black rubberised torch.

'Look at the side of his garden wall; there's a path going up the side that cuts through to the street behind. We could sneak up there and try to look over his wall and see if we can see what's going on. If we see them coming out with a bag of stuff then we can call the police and report the burglary anonymously or else we might see if they've been invited inside and find out if Milton Scott is involved.'

'Brilliant! Why didn't I think of that?' he said as he opened the door. 'Let's go.' They both jumped out of the van and ran, or as much like running as they could manage, over the road and onto the path up the side of Milton Scott's property. Abigail looked back and noticed Alasdair lagging behind,

'Come on Alasdair,' she shouted back in a whisper, 'keep up!'

'I've got a bad back, I'm not bent over like this for speed you know!' Abigail stopped a little further on and surveyed the wall. It was six feet high and covered in moss, with a rounded top; not easy to get at to see over the top of it. Alasdair came wheezing up next to her.

'Oh God, I'm going to be laid-up for a week after this. How are we going to see what's going on? I could crouch down and you could stand on my back to look over?'

'Yep, I can see that working Alasdair, the state your back's in. I'll get down on my hands and knees and you look over the wall.' She got down on the ground ready for Alasdair to do his bit but he hesitated. 'Come on Alasdair, we'll miss it!'

'Oh Abby, it doesn't seem right. I can't possibly...'

Abigail glared round at him. 'It doesn't seem right that I'm having to put my hands in this mud but I'm doing it, now please get up there.' Alasdair stepped gingerly up on her back, one foot on her coccyx and the other on her shoulders to spread his weight, and slowly peered over the top of the wall. 'Are you OK there Abby?'

Abigail braced herself against his weight. 'Fine, but you're having skinny lattes from now on. What can you see?' Alasdair stared intently towards the house whose rear was not quite as grand and imposing as the front. Typical, he thought, all show and bluster at the front but just normal once you get past the façade. The light was on in the kitchen window, just next to the back door, and he could see people moving around inside.

'I can see them but I don't know what's going on. Terrible kitchen though, one of those modern stainless steel affairs; I've always said they shouldn't be allowed to put those in period houses.'

Abigail was straining under his weight. 'I'll alert the editor at *Homes and Garden* magazine, now what are they doing?' Through the kitchen window he could see two men sitting at a centre island. They both had blue overalls on and seemed to be talking to someone that Alasdair couldn't see.

'They're definitely invited guests; they're having coffee I think, not robbing him anyway. Hang on,' he leaned over to try and see more clearly. 'Oh my God Abby, he's there, I can see Milton, he's giving them something but I can't see what it is.'

'That would seem to be fairly damning then, what else?'

'Just talking I think. Oh hell!' He jumped down, breathing heavily. 'I think they might have seen me. Milton turned and looked out of the window right in this direction.'

Abigail got up and wiped her hands on her trousers. 'He won't have seen you, not looking from a lit room out into the dark, I'm pretty sure of it. We should go anyway, we've got what we needed. It seems clear that they know each other and maybe he was paying them for their work?' They started walking back down the pathway towards the van.

'I bet that's it, payment for their ill-gotten gains. We're going to have to report this to the police.'

'I told you we can't! We'll end up in a lot of trouble if we do that given how we got the information. No, if we're going to get him caught we're going to have to be a little bit cleverer than that.' They climbed into the van and Abigail started the engine, pulling off from the roadside. 'I'll drop you off at home and then I'm getting the van back to the library before anyone finds out about this. We'll talk tomorrow.'

Chapter Twenty-Five

Abigail woke at seven thirty the next morning despite having had only four hours sleep, but the adrenalin was still coursing through her veins. She had been having a strange dream that she was back at her school disco but the music had been speeded up, as if someone was playing old thirty-three-speed records at the seventy-eight setting on the record player.

The sun was pushing its way into the room through a crack in the curtains, and the birds chirping outside suggested another fine day ahead. Last night, she had come home and gone straight upstairs before undressing and throwing her clothes over the old armchair in her bedroom and flopping into bed. Now, looking at her jacket on the arm of the chair she could see two muddy imprints from a pair of size eight boots. I can't believe we did that last night, she thought as she put on her dressing gown, we must have been mad. But it did get us some information and I've got to hand it to Alasdair; his feelings about Milton Scott were borne out, which just shows he's not as barmy as I sometimes think. I'm surprised he hasn't called yet, he must be turning cartwheels at home, not to mention Sophie who'll be wondering how on earth he's ended up involved in this now.

Emma was pottering about in the kitchen when Abigail came in for breakfast. 'Morning Abigail, you're up early. I wasn't expecting you for hours yet. How did it go last night?' Abigail relayed the story of their surveillance expedition as Emma gradually stopped what she was doing and became more engrossed in the story until she was sitting at the table opposite Abigail hanging on to every detail. 'Bloody hell, that's incredible. What did the police say about it?'

'That's the problem, we can't tell the police. We borrowed the mobile library without permission; goodness knows what they'd say about that. I'd lose my job, let alone what the police would do to us for spying.'

'Could they do anything? I mean you were just parked on a public road and then the path up the back of the house was public as well wasn't it?'

'Well, yes, but I'd still be more worried about taking the library van. They might arrest me for grand theft auto.'

Emma squinted. 'Do we have that here? I thought that was just an American thing. We'd probably have something like, taking a vehicle without permission. Our crimes never sound as grand as they do in America.'

'Oh hang on,' Abigail rose from her chair and went through to the lounge, returning a few seconds later with a paperback book in her hand, on the cover of which Emma could see a large eye peering through a magnifying glass and a trilby hat on top of one of the words in the title. 'I ended up with this book from Alasdair. He was getting into it with his usual gusto last night, full detective rig out, you can imagine.' Emma nodded and smiled, as she could perfectly well imagine how he had looked. Abigail handed her the book. 'I had a flick through it and it's been written by an American so some of the references are from over there. Quite an interesting book though I must say.' She poured them each a mug of tea and sat down again.

'So did you put a tail on the van?' Emma said only half joking.

'No, we did not. I've no idea what we do next, we need to try and get some proper evidence for the police without getting into trouble ourselves.'

'What's Alasdair thinking about it all?'

'I've not spoken to him yet this morning, but knowing him

he'll be putting a call into Downing Street to get the SAS to storm the building. I think we need to do something more subtle but equally as effective.' She took the book from Emma. 'Perhaps the answer lies within?' she said, waving the book in the air, just as the phone started to ring in the hallway. 'Ah, speak of the devil, that'll be Columbo on the phone now!'

Alasdair lay flat on his back on the bathroom floor, the miasma of the family remedy wafting up from his back into his nostrils and, he wasn't sure, but he could have sworn there was a greenish cloud wafting across the ceiling towards the extractor fan. This is definitely the stuff, he thought, I wish I'd started marketing this years ago. I could have done for backs what Dr Scholl did for feet – Mr Mills' Lumber Wonder. Perhaps I could get a doctorate from the university to make it sound better.

The phone sat on the floor next to him, ringing loudly on the speakerphone since it was too much effort trying to keep the handset to his ear while maintaining optimum back relief. Abigail answered on the fifth ring. 'Abby! How are you this morning? Hope you're none the worse for wear. I'm laid-up on the floor again with my back!'

'Good God, you've got it on speaker phone.' Abigail jerked the phone from her ear. 'You need to turn it down Alasdair, it sounds like you're in a cave with a megaphone. You'll do my eardrums a mischief.' He fumbled with the phone and managed to turn the volume up at first, thereby allowing Emma, who was twenty feet from Abigail's phone, to partake in the conversation, but then turning it down again to a more reasonable level. 'How's that now?'

'Much better. I take it your back didn't react well to our expedition last night?'

'No, it's seized up completely. When I got up this morning I had to come straight to the bathroom and lie down. Sophie's not pleased at all with this caper, she thinks we should stay out of the way of it all. Not to mention the difficulty she had when she was trying to get ready this morning with a sleeping policeman in the bathroom, pardon the pun.' He tried to raise himself up to a sitting position but failed as pain stabbed him in the back. 'Nope, just tried moving and it's still agony. This is extremely inconvenient, we'll need to wait until later to go round and confront him.'

Abigail's heart leapt. 'Whoa, what do you mean "confront him"? We'll do no such thing, I've just been chatting about it with Emma and we need to find some way to implicate him to the police. We can't go charging in throwing accusations around. We don't have any proof.'

'But we saw them there Abby, we've as good as got him banged to rights! The van that was seen outside my house when the burglary took place was in his driveway and he was talking to the people who were in it.' He winced as pain shot up his back again due to the tension in his body.

Abigail's voice was calm when it came back over the speaker. 'OK then, Columbo, so we go to the police and tell them about it and we show them what? The photographs we took last night, the video from our surveillance cameras? Or perhaps a quick sketch we can draw on the back of a napkin? If we go to the police we'll look daft. We've no proof and they know you and Milton don't get on so it just looks like you're trying to throw some mud at him.'

Alasdair sighed heavily. 'Maybe. But we did see them there, surely that counts for something?'

'It counts enough to let us know that our hunch, or rather your hunch, was right. But we don't know that the van that we saw last night is the same one that was at your house – we didn't get the registration. The one Dorothy saw may have been stolen and used for the burglary, we don't know.'

Alasdair was prepared to concede there was some logic to this but his frustration was still evident.

'OK, Abby. But I know it was him, I can sense it. I mean it's not as if they were making a business call at that time to check his guttering, is it?' Abigail had to concede this time that he did have a point. 'And they were having coffee with him as well so my gut feeling is it's him behind this, and I'm going to make sure that my property is returned.'

It was Abigail's turn to sigh. 'Yes, you may be right Alasdair. But let's not do anything rash, we need to figure this one out. Let's not put him on the most wanted list as public enemy number one just yet.'

'Public enemy number one? Have you got my book Abby?' He could almost feel the heat from her face coming down the line.

'Erm no, well yes, but never mind about that. Just you get your back sorted out and I'll see what I can find out. I'll talk to you later.'

Chapter Twenty-Six

Sophie stood in the King's Park surrounded by activity, which, if she were being honest (and she was always apt to be), was completely bewildering. She'd started up some giant machine and it was gaining momentum. Hopefully not running out of steam too soon, she thought. From her position in the middle of the grass, she looked at the two large marquees, bunting strung along the top of their open fronts. Inside they were laid out with row upon row of tables and chairs, ready to cater for the throngs of people looking to partake of their high tea. Large flower displays would be placed on the tables on the morning of the day in question and volunteers would be bustling back and forth serving the food. Facing the marquees was a row of small stalls, which had been set up for various charities that would be raising funds for their causes, or simply just raising awareness. On Sunday, where she stood now would be adorned with further rows of chairs for the audience to sit and watch the concert on the stage, which was being erected before her very eyes.

Around twenty people in jeans, work shirts and toolbelts scurried around like ants, each one knowing where to be and when, in order to secure the next piece of the stage. She gazed absently at the lights and speakers being hoisted onto the gantry above and tried to summon up the energy to get on with the next thing on her 'to do' list, but, for the moment, that energy escaped her. She sat down at one of the tables just inside the main marquee and stretched her legs out. The tiredness had been lurking in the shadows for a few days now and she had fended it off, but now it seeped into her bones, leaving her feeling exhausted. The pressure upon her to oversee the event was more than enough, but to top it all off, Alasdair was now getting involved in moonlight adventures and goodness knows what else and it was all just too exhausting. Just as she thought this her mobile phone rang and Alasdair's name flashed up on the screen. 'Hello,' she answered flatly, not being particularly enamoured to speak to him at the moment.

'Sophie, where are you? You sound a bit off; you must be tired. Why don't you come home for lunch and we can have some wine?'

'I somehow think that's more likely to tire me out even further. I have things to be doing anyway – I do have a lot going on at the moment you know.' There was a moment's silence on the other end of the phone.

'I'm sorry for waking you up this morning. It was just such a huge shock, I thought you'd be keen to know what we'd discovered. Especially with him being . . .'

'Don't even say it, Alasdair,' Sophe said frostily. 'I'm well aware he's acting as our main guest on Sunday but given that you have absolutely no proof of anything, I'm not going to change things now! You just seem to be intent on trying to blame him for this but it's getting out of hand. And as for dragging Abigail into all this, well. Although I thought she would have had more sense.'

'But we saw him speaking to the people who burgled our house!'

'No, you didn't. You saw him talking to people, that's all. It could have been completely above board, nothing to do with our burglary.'

Alasdair let out a high-pitched yowl. 'Oh come on Sophie, they turned up at his house in the early hours of the morning, that's not normal!'

'No, maybe not, but it's not against the law either. In fact, if we want to start going down that road it's far more suspicious and strange to steal a library van and sit out in it in the street staring at someone's house. Isn't that called stalking? You need to get a grip of yourself Alasdair; Milton Scott is not a criminal!' She stabbed her finger onto the phone and cut off the call before he had a chance to reply. Honest to God, she thought, this is getting out of hand.

'Good morning Mrs Mills.' Sophie jerked her head round and saw Milton Scott standing over her, holding two takeaway coffees, one of which he held out to her. 'I was buying one for myself,' he gestured towards the small shop just inside the park, 'and I thought you might like one.' Sophie wondered how long he'd been standing there and how much of her conversation he had heard. He was studying her quite carefully and her face must have given something away. 'Sorry to interrupt your phone call, I couldn't help overhear that you sounded a bit annoyed. Not a problem with the plans I hope?'

'No, all fine, just my husband causing difficulties again. It's nothing.' She took the coffee and sipped at it. 'It's very kind of you Mr Scott, thank you.'

He smiled and shrugged. 'It's no problem.' He sat down at the table and sipped his coffee while he watched the work on the stage. 'It didn't sound like nothing, if you don't mind me saying? If there's anything I can do to help then I'd be happy to do so.' He smiled at her again, although she noticed it lacked any real warmth and he was still studying her intently. Did he hear what I said, she wondered. He might have but then why not mention it? Maybe he's trying to save causing me any embarrassment. I mean if I was in his shoes I'd want to know what was being said about me but I suppose in his position you maybe get used to it. Such a shame people don't give him more of chance.

She pointed to the stage. 'What do you think of the Milton Scott Stage?' He regarded it for a few moments, stroking his chin thoughtfully.

'It looks impressive. So when would you like to go over the schedule for Sunday? I'd like to have a day or two to let it settle in my mind and make sure I'm properly prepared for my opening and closing speeches.'

'Oh, we could do that now if you have time? I have the schedule in my bag.' He nodded amiably and she leaned down to rifle through the folder in her bag for the schedule, unaware that he was still stroking his chin thoughtfully, but now staring at her and wondering just exactly how much he had to worry about over what he had heard.

Chapter Twenty-Seven

Abigail was sitting in her lounge with the newspaper on her lap but staring instead out of the window, her mind racing. I haven't felt this awake for months, she thought, it's like being given an electric jolt. I can't believe that he's got me involved in this but I must say I do love having something to work my brain properly. I believe this is what would be termed a three-pipe problem in Mr Holmes' day.

Emma had been upstairs getting ready to go to the restaurant, since she was working this afternoon as it was the grand opening tonight. She had thought it odd to open on a Thursday rather than a Saturday but as Alec had pointed out, you don't want to open a restaurant and have a baptism of fire with a big crowd on a Saturday night. Better to open quietly without any fanfare and iron out any wrinkles before starting to advertise and pull in the customers. With High Tea in the Park on Sunday, they were also hopeful to pick up some business from the influx of people to the town then, so a couple of days to settle in were just ideal. So open they would, and if any customers came by then it would be an opportunity to see how they could cope, and to grease the wheels of commerce, a free bottle of wine would be given to each table who wished it, free coffees to those who didn't. She came into the lounge, throwing her jacket over a chair and sitting down on the sofa.

'All ready for the big night?' Abigail asked.

'I think so,' she looked a little uncertain, 'it's such a new thing for me, well for Alec as well, and we're just hoping it goes well. Fingers crossed. By the time we open later we'll be all hands on deck.'

Abigail smiled. 'Ship shape and Bristol fashion. I'm not sure what that means exactly but Arthur used to say it and it seemed to be a good thing.' She opened the paper and casually flicked through the pages, not really taking in the stories. 'You know what puzzles me, Emma? If Milton Scott has such a successful business and is a wealthy man, why would he get involved in this sort of thing, assuming that he is involved? I mean this website he's got going must be raking in a good bit of money, just look at the size of the house he bought. It must easily have cost over a million pounds.

'True,' Emma said, 'but then aren't these people always in debt up to the hilt to finance their lifestyle? He might have a big house but it doesn't mean he's wealthy. Maybe his business isn't doing as well as he'd like everyone to think.' Abigail thought back to how Alasdair had described the interior of the house – decadently distasteful he had said in typical style. A lot of furniture but much of it was either in poor repair or seemed to be imitation. She had just put it down to him being younger and not having good taste but then one did have to ask if there was more to it than that.

'But what would he then have to gain by stealing the slippers from Alasdair? It's not as if that's helping his situation in any way is it?'

Emma chuckled. 'Maybe he's put them on eBay to get some cash.' Abigail stared at her.

'What? I'm only joking Abigail.'

'No, but what if you're right?' Abigail said shaking her head. 'What if he stole them to sell on and get the money – Alasdair paid eight thousand pounds for them and there were a few collectors after them so I bet one of them would love to get them at a discount.'

'But what would be the point of that, they would be stolen goods so whoever bought them could never tell anyone they had them or show them off. It would seem a bit pointless to me.'

'That's true,' Abigail said getting up and going over to the sideboard, bringing out an old stamp album, 'but let's not forget what sort of people we're dealing with here.'

'Criminals?' Emma offered

'No,' said Abigail, 'collectors.'

She sat down next to Emma and flipped through the album. 'Look at all these, dozens of different stamps, literally hundreds of hours spent on it and these never saw the light of day or went on display. Arthur was a collector, and that's the thing. For him and whoever might buy those slippers, it's not about being able to show them off, it's to satisfy the urge to complete the collection. I saw it in Arthur when he had to find one stamp to complete some part of his album; it was like an itch that wouldn't go away. Looking for it in antique fairs, stamp collector fairs, junk shops; anywhere there were likely to be stamps he would spend hours trying to find it. It must be a genetic thing I think – either you have that or you don't.'

Emma frowned. 'So you think Milton Scott might have sold the slippers to help to keep himself in the manner to which he's become accustomed?'

Abigail raised an inquisitive eyebrow. 'It's possible isn't it? I mean from what I've read about him he didn't come from money, his parents were normal working-class folk. I think he likes to trade on the fact of being in the same family tree as Sir Walter Scott but then look what happened there – maybe Milton Scott doesn't want history to repeat itself.'

'Why, what happened to Sir Walter Scott?' Emma asked.

'He had great wealth and then lost it in some bad investments and was saddled with huge debts. He spent the last years of his life trying to earn enough money to pay it all back, but he died in the process, still down on his uppers. Maybe it's the family curse.'

Chapter Twenty-Eight

Emma left for work just after two, leaving Abigail chewing things over in her mind. She was back in her chair again flipping through pages, although this time it was *The Detective's Handbook* as opposed to the *Stirling Observer*. I wonder what the next step would be, she wondered. This is all just supposition at the moment so I can't go to the police, or could I? Would they just think it was my imagination running riot or do they have to follow it up? I'm not sure I want to start some sort of investigation into him when we don't have any proof – I'll end up being charged with wasting police time. I'm not even sure it's a good idea to tell Alasdair about all this given there's a fair chance he'll do something hasty, although it is his thing and it might be best to have a sounding board for my idea.

She put on her coat and picked up the phone in the hallway on her way out, ringing ahead to see if Alasdair was still there. He was, but still sounding in quite a bit of pain, but in any case she was to come around the back and let herself in – Sophie had left the door unlocked in case of an emergency. It was another fine day and as she came to the end of her garden path she spotted the familiar ginger figure of Waffles walking further up the road. She was about to turn in the opposite direction to go to Alasdair's house when she stopped and turned in time to see Waffles' tail swishing around the bend in the road. She suddenly started walking after him – I wonder where you're going, she thought. Let's find out if you've got a home or if you are a stray looking for someone to take you in. If you were a suspect then I would follow you and check what your movements were, so you can be my test subject. She walked quickly up the path, crossing into the road at one point to see further ahead past the bend in the road, and there was Waffles padding casually towards the end of the road. She quickened her pace, keeping him in sight at all times but also staying a safe enough distance back so as not to be caught. Chapter five, she remembered, and if I can follow a cat with their heightened senses and awareness then following a person should be easy.

Waffles stopped ahead of her and sat down looking around, and instinctively Abigail pressed herself into the wall to prevent him from seeing her – chapter five, section two, avoiding detection. If she had been on the tail of someone this would have looked completely suspicious of course but then, she thought, you have to adapt the methods to suit the target. I'm rather enjoying this now. She crept up the path, keeping in close to the wall, trying to avoid being jagged on the head by hawthorn bushes coming over the top, and she saw Waffles turn and saunter into a garden. Damn, I'm going to lose him – she jogged along but couldn't see him anywhere. He must live in that house, although what if that's only his shortcut home? She walked briskly around the end of the road and into the street behind, and sure enough there he was walking towards another house before sitting on the doorstep and miaowing loudly. This had the desired effect of making the door magically open, at least it must be magic for a cat, and in he went. Abigail felt strangely proud of herself that she had successfully followed the subject without being rumbled and found out the information she was after, albeit the subject was a cat, but you had to start somewhere. She walked past Waffles' home and back around to head in the direction of Alasdair's house.

She let herself in the back door and walked through the kitchen and hall to the bottom of the stairs. 'Alasdair? Are you up there?'

An echoing voice shouted back. 'Yes, same place I've been all morning. Could you make me a sandwich, I'm starving!'

'I can do, what would you like?'

The echoing voice again. 'I'd love a fried egg, keep the yolk runny please.' Abigail took a step towards the kitchen then stopped.

'Isn't that going to be fraught with difficulty if you're lying on your back on the floor? It'll just run all over you. I'll see if you've got any cold meat.'

'Not more corned beef!' he shouted back as she walked off into the kitchen.

Ten minutes later, Alasdair was chewing a ham and mustard sandwich with great enthusiasm, and a glass of milk with a bent over straw sat on the floor next to his head. Abigail was standing outside the door, a hankie pressed over her nose and mouth. 'How much of that stuff have you put on? It's foul.'

Alasdair stopped munching his sandwich and looked over. 'This stuff as you call it is a wonder medicine, I'll be up and about in no time. I accept that it's a trifle aromatic but then that's all the rage these days isn't it? I could sell this as one of those aroma air fresheners for people with colds, clear their sinuses right up. This has dozens of uses, Abby – I can't believe my family never cashed in on it before. This will make my fortune.' Abigail pulled the chair over from the landing and sat down, still outside the bathroom door.

'I wouldn't order the private jet just yet,' she said, 'I take it Sophie is away out sorting some things for the high tea? She must just love you being laid-up at a time when she could do with your help.'

Alasdair finished his sandwich and took a long drink of his milk. 'I know, I do feel bad about it, but she'll understand. Although she was a bit short with me this morning – tired I think. I don't think she's on board with our investigation you know.'

'Well, can you blame her? She's run herself ragged organising this event and now, just as it's about to happen, we're both grabbing the end of a very big rug and trying to pull it out from under her. Still, Emma and I were discussing things this morning and I've come up with a theory. I assume you'll want to hear it?'

Alasdair listened intently, his head laid back on a chequered cushion on the floor, pondering the details as Abigail relayed what she and Emma had discussed that morning.

'My God Abigail, that could be it. Why not? I've heard stranger things when I was a solicitor. He had that court case with Revenue and Customs a few years back which suddenly disappeared and we assumed that he had been cleared. Maybe he agreed to pay out what he was due them and it was settled. From what I recall at the time it was a sizeable sum they were after; he might be in debt after that. But then what about his business? That website he's got seems to be doing rather well given the house he bought?'

Abigail shook her head. 'Not necessarily, as Emma said he could be funding it all on further credit or loans somehow. Anyway, I looked at his website and he only charges three pounds fifty for a valuation on an item. It would take a hell of a lot of things being valued to pay for that house and his lifestyle.'

Alasdair nodded, conceding that it would seem unlikely. 'So we need to try and find out more about his website and perhaps about him too? If we can get some background information on him then we'll be better able to gauge how to tackle this.'

Abigail smiled. 'Chapter seven, I believe?'

He laughed and nodded. 'I believe so. Now how are we going to go about this? We don't want to tip him off that we're checking into him.'

'So we won't ask anyone locally, that way he won't pick up any gossip or, dare I say it, word on the street. We'll just Google him; loads of stuff will come up I'm sure.'

Alasdair held up a hand, his brow furrowing. 'But if he's the technical whizz that's been reported before, could he find out somehow if we're checking him online? I bet he's got some way to monitor if he's being looked up, especially if he's involved in dirty deeds. Don't they do that with worms or something that they send out? I'm sure I read about that somewhere.'

'No idea Alasdair, but it's a fair point. But how do you find anything out these days without a computer? It's impossible. We don't exactly have time to travel around the country asking questions.' They sat in silence for a few minutes trying to figure out some solution. Abigail then stood up, 'Sorry Alasdair, I need to get to work, I've got to help out this afternoon. We've got a visitor coming from another library to show us the new . . .' she stopped, gazing off into space for a second. Alasdair watched her.

'Yes? What is it?'

'Eureka!' she pushed the chair back against the wall. 'I've just had my eureka moment. I'll tell you later, got to go!' She turned and nipped down the stairs as Alasdair's voice echoed after her.

'Abby! You can't leave me here like this, I need to know what's going on, and I need some help getting up and if nothing else, I'd like another sandwich!'

Chapter Twenty-Nine

Alec was standing on the pavement outside the restaurant when Emma arrived. He was gesturing to two men up ladders who were heaving a large sign into position. Another man was standing next to him, who Emma couldn't quite see yet, but was presumably a third member of the sign company team. From where she was the sign looked very good indeed. It was done in an old-fashioned style with a black background and gold lettering in a simple yet classic hand depicting the name of the restaurant. Hanging out at right angles from the building was a metal sign, which was carved into the shape of a man holding what looked like a bread paddle and aiming it towards the door in a round furnace. The sign was black apart from the area inside the open door of the furnace, which had been painted to look like a blazing fire, on which the puddings would no doubt be cooking along nicely. It was like the style of sign that would have hung outside an apothecary or blacksmith's in olden days.

As Emma drew close she shouted out to Alec, 'Looks good, we're now ready for business!' As she did so he turned around revealing the face of the man standing next to him and Emma stopped in her tracks. It was John. What in hell's name did he want hanging around here apart from looking to cause trouble? Alec smiled and waved her over.

'Hi Emma. I think I might have found our first customer for tonight.' She walked over, her face now red with anger, and stood facing John.

'What the hell do you want?' He gave a look of mock distress towards Alec and held up his hands apologetically.

'Hey, calm down. I was just passing and saw the new place so I wanted to have a look. I didn't know you worked here – I take it you're the cleaner, are you?' He fixed her eyes and held them with a cold stare, which she thought he must have been practicing in front of the mirror. He then turned to Alec, 'I hope you don't let her speak to all of the customers like this,' he said.

'Oh come on John, this place isn't something you'd be seen dead in – you knew I worked here and you're out to cause bother. Alec, we need to bar this idiot right away, he'll ruin opening night.'

Alec turned to John and smiled. 'Sorry about this, like I was saying, feel free to come along tonight and help us celebrate the opening.' Alec smiled graciously, still watching Emma.

'You know I think I might just do that. Anyway, bye for now.' He walked forward towards her and instinctively she moved aside and then immediately cursed herself for letting him past rather than making him walk around her. She gave Alec a blazing look and then marched into the restaurant, giving the two men up the ladder a similar look in return for their furtive glances. Alec came in after her.

'What on earth was that all about? I assume that there's a history but we can't afford to go alienating potential customers. You mind telling me what the story is?' He pulled a chair out at one of the tables and gestured to it before sitting on the opposite side, waiting expectantly. Emma sat down and gave Alec the gory details of her life with the deplorable John. He seemed to be understanding enough but his face was still looking grim.

'We can't have any bother here tonight Emma, not on our opening night. It just takes a bad opening and word gets around, I hope you realise that?'

She nodded. 'I can't help it if he comes here but hopefully he won't – it's not exactly his type of place. I won't let him walk all over me again though, but I'll not let anything happen if I can help it.' She got up and went back to the kitchen to start checking the deliveries that had come in today, and in her head a small light came on. She dug her mobile phone out of her pocket and then went out of the back door to make a call.

Chapter Thirty

At the library Valerie Stewart was sitting at a computer with a pleasant young man who was eagerly pointing out things on the screen and explaining the brave new world which was coming to their online services. Abigail smiled as she walked past, and thankfully a customer was standing at the returns desk thereby preventing Valerie from roping her into their discussion. Once she had dealt with the customer, the library was quiet and so Abigail sat down at one of the other computer screens and brought up a list of all of the libraries in the country. Scrolling down the list there was page after page of names, addresses and contact details for the public libraries in the United Kingdom. She was still trying to figure out in her head the best way to go about this. She knew what she wanted to do but just wasn't quite sure how to do it without seeming either mad or raising too many questions. If I send an email to all of the libraries and ask them to check their local newspapers for any article on Milton Scott then I could get some information which could be useful. Although I don't want anyone to search on the internet for the details in case that still triggers off any alert that he might be able to see. She sat back on her chair and closed her eyes for a moment before a smile came across her face and she leaned forward again and started typing a new email:

Dear Colleagues,

My name is Abigail Craig and I work at the library in the wonderful
city of Stirling. We have been approached here by the regional police
headquarters for our help in a project which they tell me is possibly
of national importance. The premise is this; what if the internet went
down due to being subjected to cyber attacks, how could they in the
police and the security services still pool news and local information
from around the country? What they have realised is that with the
library network across the country, we are already the gatekeepers for
a huge amount of information, both local and national, and in times of
emergency if the library network were to be mobilised to collate local
information and keep a central point advised then the overall picture
in the country could still be tracked.

I'm sure I don't have to tell you that in an age when we in the
libraries are under increasing threat from cutbacks and online services,
it is an honour that one of the true values of our own service has
been realised, not to mention the key role we play in education and
introducing our next generations to literature and knowledge.

The police have requested that we contact all of you and ask you
to carry out the following test, by way of manual means only. This
could be through local word of mouth or with your resources of
local newspapers which are routinely gathered at the moment. The
information they have requested, which has been randomly selected
as a test, is thus:

- Check for any information in your area from the last six months on
  a businessman by the name of Milton Scott.
- Check for any information in your area from the last six months on
  antiques or collectible items being stolen in your local areas.

When you have checked this, the articles are to be copied and emailed
back to us here so that we can collate and pass them back to the police
headquarters. Since we are competing with the internet, and not to
mention because it is a chance for us to display just how valuable we
are, they have asked us to respond by tomorrow noon to see how the
network can perform.

Good luck to you all and let's show them what we can do!

> Yours sincerely,
> Abigail Craig
> Senior Librarian, Stirling Library

Abigail read over the email, wondering if this was just getting a little out of hand now that she was involving the entire country in their madness. But, at the same time, if this got them the information they needed to prove or disprove their theory then it would be worth it. Abigail spun her chair around and watched as the young man was still pointing out new things on the computer screen and telling Valerie how the future of the library would be secured by providing more services online to the public. Valerie glanced over towards Abigail, an exasperated look on her face and her eyes pleading for help. Abigail picked up the cue and let out a painful groan, stopping the man mid–sentence, and he turned to face her. She gave him her best pained expression, not altogether unconvincing although to the casual onlooker it would be difficult to know if it was a heart attack or constipation, which perhaps added to its strength. 'I'm sorry Valerie, I'll have to go to the doctor about this pain, remember I was telling you about it?'

'Oh yes Abigail, I remember,' she would have been a natural in an amateur dramatics performance. 'Off you go and I can handle things here. I think Mr Bristow is just about finished now?' They both looked at him and he looked from one to the other.

'Erm, well I could go on . . .'

Valerie stood up. 'I'm sure, however we're just about to get to our busy time with the kids coming in after school so we'll need to call it a day. I'll get your coat.' She hurriedly helped him on with his coat and showed him down the steps and on to the street, before he really knew what was happening.

Abigail laughed as she came back in. 'We'll never get to heaven Val.'

'Nope. So what were you beavering away on there?'

'Just some information I need from the other libraries, nothing special, just a project I'm working on. There might be some emails in for me tomorrow morning just in case you get them before me.' Valerie eyed her suspiciously but Abigail scooped up her coat before she could ask further and said goodbye, then stepped out onto the street.

Chapter Thirty-One

For the moment there didn't feel like there was much more to be done as Abigail stepped outside the library. She glanced left and saw the road leading down the hill past the Albert Halls and in the direction of home. Not too appealing a thought at the moment as Emma would be out and with everything going on she felt that she wanted to be among people rather than sitting at home on her own. The world was starting to feel like an exciting place again, not to mention a little dangerous, which she found not a little invigorating. She looked to her right and saw the statue of William Wallace standing on top of the building at the top of King Street. She tried not to let her gaze fall on the grey monstrosity which stood behind it, a legacy of the seventies building craze to use concrete and build purely for function. How such a building had ever been allowed in the centre of a historic town like Stirling was beyond her. She gave a small involuntary sigh and headed off to her right and down into the town. As she came down King Street towards the shopping centre she glanced inside the Burgh coffee shop and saw the familiar figure of Sophie Mills sitting on one of the stools in the window, lost in thought, her hands clasped around a coffee cup. Abigail waved but Sophie was staring off into the distance, blissfully unaware of anything happening outside her own thoughts. Abigail went in and ordered a vanilla latte at the counter and then went to sit down next to Sophie. 'Hi there, how's you?' Sophie looked around and slowly came out of herself, like someone being brought round from hypnosis.

'Sorry Abigail, I was miles away there. What are you doing here?'

'Well coffee mainly, but I thought we could have a chat. You looked like you had the weight of the world on your shoulders there.' The young barista, whom Abigail took to be a student, brought over her latte and placed it in front of her. The smell of vanilla wafted into her nose, forcing her to take a sip and she nodded her head with satisfaction. 'Shall we get a comfier seat?' she asked. They both decamped from the stools in the window and took one of the sofas in the main part of the café. 'So how's things looking for Sunday? The weather seems to be co-operating for once.'

'True, the forecast is good. I think everything's in place, we've got the stage and marquees built now and the sound check is tomorrow afternoon and then we should be all ready. It's just . . .' She tailed off and looked down at her cup.

'What's wrong Soph? It's not like you to be down. You should be on top of the world at the moment. Sunday's going to be the biggest event we've had here for years, decades even, and you've organised it to the smallest detail. Although, I'm imagining there may be one fly in the ointment at the moment?' Sophie looked at her. 'I mean Alasdair. He isn't trying to cause problems, nor am I for that matter since I seem to be mixed up in it too.'

Sophie turned and faced her. 'Abigail, we've known each other for quite a few years now. Tell me, is there anything to all this business with Milton? I keep thinking that it must be Alasdair off on one of his tangents but when I see you taking it seriously I start to wonder. What's your gut feeling on it all?'

'Well,' Abigail exhaled loudly, 'to be honest I thought it was a lot of rubbish as well when it first started – just Alasdair trying to occupy himself – and, well, he obviously doesn't like Milton Scott.' Sophie nodded. 'But the more I think about it, I can't help thinking it might just be possible.' She put a hand onto Sophie's. 'Sorry.'

Sophie waved her arms. 'Oh, it's not your fault Abby, in fact if it turns out to be true then it's not Alasdair's fault either but . . .' she looked exasperated, 'I should have known it would be too good for it all to go smoothly. I don't want everything to be attached to some scandal.'

'Look Sophie, it might well be that he's not involved and in any case, what if we wait until after the high tea before we do anything about contacting the police? I'm waiting to get some emails back tomorrow to see if I can find out some things about our Mr Scott which may help answer some questions but its Saturday tomorrow, so what could possibly happen between then and Sunday? Even if we do get any information it'll take some time to sort out and we can easily wait until Monday before we make our next move. How does that sound?'

Sophie looked a little more relaxed but her brow was still furrowed. 'I suppose. But what if Milton is arrested afterwards, won't it tar the memory of the day when it turns out he's a criminal?'

'I don't think so, you weren't to know. If anything it will just make him look worse for taking everyone in and trying to play lord of the manor when he's been up to no good.' She smiled, trying to look reassuring. 'See? It'll be fine, I'm sure of it.'

Chapter Thirty-Two

At The Pudding Furnace, the afternoon flew by in a blur of menus, wine lists, tablecloths, food preparation and in general running around like mad getting every last detail in place for six o'clock when the doors would open for the first time. The assistant chef whom Alec had hired was busy in the kitchen and a couple of young waiters from an agency were setting the tables and doing a grand job out front.

Emma had been in better humour as the afternoon wore on and she and Alec had just passed each other by as they went back and forth around the place taking care of their allotted tasks. Now, as the moment of truth arrived, they both found a few minutes to sit down and survey their surroundings before it all changed and the public were invited in to join them. 'It's all looking good,' Alec said, 'we should be really proud of ourselves, even if I do say so myself.' Emma looked around and nodded, smiling.

'Absolutely. Hopefully everyone out there will feel as excited about it as we do and we, or rather you, will have a huge success.'

'Now, it's been a team effort. I couldn't have done it without you. I think we make quite a good team. Hopefully we won't be too busy tonight but I hope folk like it. You hear all sorts of stories of disasters on opening night. We might not get any customers at all!'

Emma squinted at him. 'Oh, I think we'll have some customers,' Alec looked worryingly at her. 'I mean there's John for a start isn't there. God help us if he turns up with his so-called friends.'

'Is that going to be awkward?' he asked, 'We can't afford to have any trouble so maybe you need to stay in the back if they do come in? From what you've told me it might not make for a pleasant time of it, under the circumstances. He clearly seems to think he's got nothing to be ashamed of?'

'That's true, but I'm here to do a job and do it I will. I'm not going to hide in the back. Anyway, as long as I'm completely professional and just do my job I'm sure it'll be fine. They'll have their food and their free wine and then they'll be off.' She gave him a reassuring smile and then looked at her watch. 'Will we get the show on the road? The proof of the, well, pudding, is in the eating after all.' Alec got up laughing nervously and walked to the door, turning the sign around from Closed to Open, and unlocking the door. Emma and the other staff, who had gathered to watch the moment, gave a small cheer and a round of applause, as all eyes then fell on the street to watch for the first customers to arrive.

The first hour was painfully quiet. A few people stopped and looked at the menu on the window but when they peered inside and saw the tables deserted they walked on, presumably not wishing to be the only ones here. Just after seven o'clock a couple who both looked around forty years old came in and were shown to a table opposite the fire which, even though only lit up with candles due to it being summer, still gave a nice cosy feel to the place. They asked about the free wine offer but instead, as they were the first, they were presented with a bottle of champagne to launch the restaurant on its maiden voyage. If not quite like the opening of the floodgates, this first couple in the restaurant did seem to encourage others to join them.

By eight o'clock there were three further tables occupied by a variety of people; an elderly couple who were celebrating an anniversary and wanted to try somewhere new, a family from France that had come here on holiday to immerse themselves in the history, and three men and a woman who seemed to be a group of friends. Alec was in the kitchen busily cooking away and the two young waiting staff were doing a grand job keeping everyone's drinks topped up and ensuring courses were moving briskly along. Emma was in the kitchen when she heard the bell above the door go off again. She skipped excitedly towards the restaurant. 'More customers, this is going to be a great night.' Her excitement came to a crunching halt as she came through and saw John and two of his undesirable friends being shown to a table by the waiter. As she stood watching them with a disgusted look on her face, John saw her and just sneered at her.

'What are you looking at?' he shouted across the room. 'Paying customers here so I want a bit of respect.' The other diners tried to look around without moving their heads, as is the British way, with only the group of friends having a better look around at the annoying behaviour. Emma went over to the table.

'Look John, if you want to come in here that's up to you, but don't ruin this. There's been a lot of hard work put in here, which I know is a concept you're not exactly familiar with, so please just button it!' She turned and marched off to the kitchen as the waiter was returning to their table with a bottle of wine, selected not for its vintage or label, but purely because it was free.

They ordered their meals and during the main course they were loud, uncouth and swore at each other as if they were sitting in the roughest of pubs, clearly doing it to try and provoke Emma. Why is it that these people can't go more than two words without swearing at each other, Emma thought as she watched them from the back of the restaurant. She didn't want to give them the satisfaction of her disappearing into the kitchen, but she didn't have any particular desire to be close to them either. Their pudding was then brought out and more wine was ordered, making them become more drunk. Alec was still working in the kitchen but keeping an eye on things and Emma could sense he was feeling that his dream of opening a nice, cosy restaurant had evaporated already.

Emma had had enough. She walked over to their table and lifted the half full bottle of wine from the table and passed it to a waiter, telling him to take it away. John was on his feet, swaying towards her. 'What the hell do you think you're playin' at? Eh? We paid for that.' Emma could feel her heart quickening but she held her ground.

'No you didn't; at least not yet, but in any case, you're upsetting the other customers and it's time you all left. Please don't come back again.' John staggered towards her but she didn't move, letting him barge into her and then send her keeling over onto the floor. He stood over her, his face flushed red and he was raging at her.

'You think because you moved away from me that you're better than me? Is that what you think, I'm goin' tae show you; you're nothin' without me. All this fancy restaurant, but I know exactly who you are!' He lunged towards her while she was still on the floor but, before he could get to her, four hands grabbed him roughly by the arms and dragged him back so fast he was lucky he didn't get whiplash. 'Hey, what the . . .' The group of friends were on their feet and now one had John with his arm up his back, face down on the floor, while the other three were standing over the table with his friends giving them a look to say, 'Just try it.' One of the men turned to Emma and helped her up from the floor.

'Are you OK?'

She brushed herself down. 'I'm fine, thanks.'

The man smiled at her. 'No problem. We're off-duty police, glad we came in now. We saw what happened and it constitutes an assault. Do you want to press charges?' Emma looked down at John squirming on the floor.

'You know I think I do. After the way he's behaved it's the least he deserves.' They all shared a quick glance with each other.

The two friends who had come with John were clearly worried judging by the look on their faces. The two policemen nearest to them turned and then bent down, giving them a quiet word to which they nodded vigorously before being sent on their way. The one who had been holding John now dragged him to his feet and out the door. The man who had helped Emma up turned towards her again.

'We'll need you to come in and make a statement tomorrow, but we'll take it from here for the moment. Shame about this; it looks like this will be a nice place, especially as I've heard you're offering a discount to the police. By the way, my name's Chris Buchan. Anyway, I hope the rest of the night will be a little calmer.' He smiled warmly at her before joining his colleagues.

Emma turned and saw the faces of the other diners watching her. 'Ladies and gentlemen, I'm very sorry for the interruption to your meals. Unfortunately the offer of free wine seems to have been too good to resist for the wrong types of people.' Everyone turned back to their tables and after an initial period of gossip about the incident, they settled back into their meals and life went on again. Alec came around the tables and topped up glasses and introduced himself and was pleased to find that the people who were there were quite prepared to put the evening down to experience and not let it put them off coming back. More people came in afterwards, filling another half dozen tables, and as the doors closed at eleven it could be said that the evening, overall at least, had been a resounding success.

Alec locked the door after letting the staff away and he and Emma sat down for a drink at one of the tables. 'Well, that went well,' he said cheerfully, 'all things considered.'

'Yeah, sorry about all that, just a bit of my past catching up with me.'

Alec shrugged. 'Well, not your fault. We've all got our baggage. I don't think it's been too bad, it was all over as quickly as it started really and no damage done thankfully. I must say it was lucky those police were here? What are the chances of that, although

I'm a little bit confused over what they were saying about a discount?'

Emma blushed slightly. 'Well, I thought it might be a nice idea, you know, support our local police, what with us having the headquarters here. Might be good business even with the small discount I proposed.'

Alec finished his whisky and laughed. 'Quite right! Now, I think we've done quite enough for today. Time for home – we'll have it all to do again tomorrow, although hopefully not quite everything!'

Chapter Thirty-Three

Alasdair woke up on Saturday morning to the faint aroma of bacon and eggs wafting through the house, which for the first time in a few days was detectable over the smell of his balm. Good old Sophie, he thought, I knew she wouldn't be mad at me for long. He gingerly swung his legs off the bed and sat on the side, his feet slipping into his tatty old slippers. Comfortable but in need of replacement; not unlike how he felt at the moment, the way his back was aching, although it was better than it had been. Still, at least he was mobile now albeit not especially quick about it. He swung his heavy, curtain fabric dressing gown on, a present from Sophie's mum, which was one of the more agreeable things she had bought for him. It resembled an old-fashioned smoking jacket, although longer, and he enjoyed the swoosh it made as he walked around the house. A man's dressing gown should be of sufficient weight and length to make a good swoosh when you turn a corner.

After a slightly slower descent of the stairs than usual, he found the kitchen to be smelling delightfully of a cooked breakfast, but no Sophie and none of it for him. The frying pan was in the sink and on the table a hastily scribbled note:

> Alasdair.
> Had to get an early start, lots to do.
> I will leave you to look after yourself.
> Back later. Sophie.

He put the note back on the table and looked around the kitchen. This place feels empty when Soph's not here. I really need to start making more of an effort to help out. With that he shuffled over to the sink and washed up the dishes that were there, carefully wiping down the worktops afterwards, aware that it was a pet hate of Sophie's that he never did this, and then checked the fridge for what he could have for breakfast. It'd be a shame to start dirtying the place again just for the sake of breakfast for one. I'll maybe just get dressed and head round to Abby's and see if she's got anything on the go. If not I'll wander into town and get something there.

As Alasdair was fiddling and cursing with two shoe horns, trying to get his socks on, Abigail was already up and out to the library. It would have been nice to have a long lie-in on her day off but she was far too anxious to see if there were any replies to her email that she had sent yesterday. No one else was at the library yet so she had the computer to herself, the quietness giving her its usual comfort. She logged in and opened up the email program and sat back waiting, and waiting, and waiting but nothing came in. She gave a sigh and went off to get a cup of tea from the kitchen. Coming back into the lending library she placed the 'Librarians do it quietly' mug, a random one taken from the kitchen, down on the desk and noticed that the screen was now filled with black text. At the bottom of the screen it read '84 new messages'. She sat gazing at them not quite believing that there had been such a response. This can't be all to do with Milton Scott surely? I thought there might be a few but not eighty-four! She picked her way through them and printed them off after checking to see if they were of any interest, which in fact nearly all of them were. They had come from as far south as Bristol and as far north as Fraserburgh, and pretty much all points in between.

There were some which gave details of the trial which had been in many of the papers, so that took up about a third of the emails. Abigail glanced at these but since they were not really what she was after she didn't go into them too deeply. But the ones that were the most intriguing were those which related to the thefts of the valuable or collectable stuff. As she read through them her mind started jumping around even more, trying to piece together what she was reading. Once they were all printed off she put them into a plastic folder and put it into her bag, before transferring all of the emails into her private folder to keep them secure. As she was heading out of the door, Bridget was coming in, trying her key in the lock and finding it open. 'Good God Abby, you nearly gave me a heart attack. I didn't expect anyone to be in yet.'

'Sorry, just came to check for replies to my email from yesterday, all done now and off home again.'

'Any luck?'

Abigail shrugged. 'Oh, you know, not bad. Anyway, I'll let you get on.' She squeezed out of the half-open door and hurried off towards the King's Park. I wonder if Alasdair's up yet, or if he can even get up. She took her mobile phone out of her bag and switched the sound back on again, noticing there was a voicemail. Even though the library wasn't even open to the public, long-held habits were hard to break and she always unconsciously put her phone on silent whenever she got there. She dialled the number for voicemail and pressed the phone to her ear, trying to listen over the traffic on the main road.

'Abby!' It was Alasdair's loud voice shouting down the phone. 'I'm at your house but you're not here, or not up, or I don't know what but I came to join you for breakfast. I'm going to have a quick walk around the block to try to ease my back off. If I'm back first I'll put a chalk mark on the door but if you're back first, well, you know. See you in a bit!' She hung up the phone and checked the time of the call. Ten minutes ago; at the speed he's walking these days, I'll be back long before he is.

Chapter Thirty-Four

Abigail put two slices of bread into the toaster and some bacon under the grill and then set out some plates and cutlery before going to look out of the bay window at the front of the lounge. After a few minutes she saw Alasdair shuffling up the street and went out to let him in. 'How's your back?' she asked.

'A little bit better,' he grimaced. 'I think the walk helped a bit. Are you just up?'

'Shhh,' Abigail said in hushed tones as she gestured him in. 'Emma's still sleeping upstairs. Late night last night at the restaurant; opening night.'

'How did it go? Did you get a free meal?' Abigail shook her head.

'No, she doesn't want anyone she knows coming yet, not until they have a few nights under their belt. I've got a table reserved for Monday night for myself, you and Sophie. Thought it might be a nice surprise and help her to relax once the high tea's over. She must be wound up like a clock this morning.'

'She was up and out before I woke up. I had to sleep in the spare room again with my back. I think she has quite a lot of meetings and final preparations to make today. Have you had breakfast yet?'

She gave him a wry glance. 'No, not yet. But it's on. Come through. I've got some news on Milton Scott which I think is very interesting.'

Abigail filled Alasdair in on her email, much to his astonishment, 'Absolutely genius, genius Abigail,' he enthused, and was even more impressed when she showed him the replies that had come back.

'Look,' she laid them out on the table, 'this one here says that a set of rare coins was stolen from a house in York. The owners had just had them valued at two thousand pounds, and then a few days later they were stolen in a break-in. Look at this bit, where they had them valued.'

Alasdair looked a little closer. 'Surprise, surprise,' he said, 'itsworthwhat.com'.

'These others are the same; although some of the rest don't actually mention the website some of them do mention that police are trying to trace a van seen in the area. Or some say the owners were hoping to sell them and it was really bad luck that they had been stolen since they needed the money to pay for a holiday or debts or some such thing. And what do you do before you sell something?'

Alasdair slapped the table. 'You get them valued. And where do you get things valued cheaply?' he asked.

'Milton's website,' Abigail replied. 'It just seems to fit. People put their stuff onto the website to get it valued, Milton or one of his cronies keeps a check for the good stuff, and then they arrange to burgle them. If they're careful and spread the jobs around the country then who's going to put two and two together between the different police forces that something bigger is going on? It's brilliant. I bet those people we saw in his house that night are the ones who burgled you and they must travel the country doing these jobs.'

Alasdair let out a whistle. 'He could be raking in a fortune when you think about some of the things people have in their homes; family heirlooms, antiques and the like. These are just the ones we've found out about but how many others didn't make it to the papers or went unnoticed when your people were checking? That's enough for me, we need to get onto the police.'

'Hang on Alasdair, I promised Sophie if we found anything out we'd wait until after the event before we go to the police.'

He looked puzzled. 'When were you speaking to Sophie?'

'Yesterday, I bumped into her in town and we had a coffee. I think she's ready to buckle under all the pressure of this you know. She's up to her eyes organising this event, which is being talked about every day on the local radio station, and now we find this out. Can you imagine? All she's worked on for the past four months is about to collapse about her ears. Unless . . .'

'What?'

'We wait. What difference will one day make? Then on Monday we can hand everything over to the police, let them take over.' Alasdair stood up and started stretching. 'That way the event goes off and is a triumph, Sophie can relax, and then Milton gets arrested.'

'But that man, that arrogant blow hard of a man still gets to lord it over everyone tomorrow. No, I can't take that. He'll be sitting up their like some sort of King and I'll know exactly what he's like. Everyone needs to know what a fraud and a criminal he is. He must have got away with this for ages!'

Abigail tried to calm him down. 'Yes, he must, and it's a terrible thing. But we're not doing this for him, we're doing it for Sophie, remember? One day won't make a huge difference. We'll tell the police we didn't come sooner because we couldn't believe it ourselves but then after seeing him on Sunday we thought it only right to go to them with our suspicions.'

Alasdair sat down again but was clearly unhappy. 'I don't know, he makes my blood boil.' Abigail gave him a stern look. 'But OK, one day and then we're dropping him in it.'

They finished up and Abigail showed Alasdair out and watched him until he walked around the corner towards his house. As she came back in and closed the front door, Emma was coming down the stairs, still in her pyjamas. 'Morning. How did things go last night?' Abigail asked.

Emma smiled. 'Oh, quite well, do you want to hear about it?'

'Absolutely. I've a bit of news to tell you myself.'

Chapter Thirty-Five

Alasdair walked slowly home, taking small steps since his back ached persistently again. I'm going to need some more balm on this today, should have known it wouldn't have got better this quickly. As he was approaching his house he heard a voice calling his name. It was Dorothy Grey waving from her lounge window and gesturing him over, and since he was without any purpose for the moment he thought it neighbourly to go over and have a chat, hopefully with a cup of tea, some cake and sympathy. The door opened as he arrived and her small eyes twinkled as she invited him in. 'Mr Mills, nice to see you. I wondered if you had any news of your slippers? You look very tired. Are you unwell?' Alasdair groaned as he slumped down into a chair.

'Mrs Grey, if I told you it all you wouldn't believe me!'

'I'll put the kettle on and you can try me, Mr Mills.' She hurried off into the kitchen and came back shortly after with two mugs of tea and a plate of chocolate biscuits. Alasdair filled her in with events thus far, both on the condition of his back, his plans for domination of the lumbar-soothing market, and last but by no means least, the story of Milton Scott and his criminal goings on. 'I don't believe it,' she said after listening for half an hour.

'I told you you wouldn't, I can scarcely believe it myself. To crown it all Abigail has agreed with my wife that we won't go to the police yet but wait until after the high tea event tomorrow. I'm almost ready to burst thinking of that man waltzing around there tomorrow when we know he's running a criminal empire across the country.' Dorothy Grey had a ponderous look on her face.

'Would we call it an empire, do we think Mr Mills? It doesn't sound like he's quite at the empire stage yet, although I do see your point about him attending the park tomorrow as the guest of honour. Not very honourable at all if you ask me.'

Alasdair snapped his fingers. 'You've hit the nail on the head there; he's not very honourable. He'll be the guest of dishonour. But what can I do about it? I promised Sophie albeit by proxy. Just need to grit my teeth and bear this one I think. Anyway, will you be coming along? It should be quite a good show by all accounts, and I'll definitely be sampling the high tea.'

Dorothy frowned. 'I'm afraid not; I don't really get out much these days so I won't be able to make it this time. I'm sure I'll hear it clearly though, since the stage looks big enough and there are enough speakers to project the music over half the city.'

Alasdair looked puzzled. 'But I thought you didn't really get out now. You've seen the stage?'

She smiled. 'Oh, not in person no, but it seems someone has deemed it wise to install a camera in the park which streams it onto the internet. It went live yesterday and I've been able to see the stage and some of the tents too. Look I'll show you.' She went over to the table in the bay window and tapped on the keys before sliding it over towards Alasdair. 'See? The picture quality is really quite good. Isn't it amazing what they can do now? It will almost feel like I'm there anyway.' Alasdair wasn't really listening, still lost in a little world of bitterness about the whole affair. Suddenly her voice caught his attention.

'What?'

'I said, isn't that Mrs Mills in the park?'

'Oh probably, I expect she'll be there all day. What's she doing?'

'Look for yourself, Mr Mills.' She turned the screen to face him and he squinted at the figure in the middle of the grass before the stage. Sophie, but not just Sophie. She was talking to the person standing very close to her, who was unmistakeably Milton Scott. Alasdair's face seemed to glide up the colour chart to a scarlet hue.

'What on earth is she doing with him! Bloody cheek.'

'Well, I'm sure they have things to go over before tomorrow, last-minute details and all that.' They watched, Alasdair still generating some heat from his face. 'Look I think they're finishing.' Sophie seemed to be walking away when Milton Scott walked after her and put a hand on her back and said one final thing before turning and walking in the other direction.

'Did he just put his hand on her as well? That's it. As if it's not bad enough that he's completely shady, he's going to start taking liberties with my wife! Well, not if I've got anything to say about it.' He started puffing and groaning, struggling to get up from his chair. 'I'm going right around there to have this out with him, once and for all.' His face had a look of complete focus and determination and he was intent on storming around there immediately. In reality, however, by the time he had gotten up from his chair and made it to the front door, the elderly Mrs Grey was waiting there holding it open for him. 'Not a word about this to anyone please Mrs Grey. I need to make a quick stop at home first and then he'll get what for!' She watched as he hobbled down the path and across the road.

Chapter Thirty-Six

'So how was the food?' Abigail asked as they were sitting at the kitchen table. 'Would you recommend it?'

'Absolutely. Proper comfort food, lots of hearty casseroles and things like that and the desserts, sorry the puddings, Alec doesn't do desserts, were to die for. You'll love it I'm sure.'

Abigail smiled. 'I'm looking forward to it. It sounds like it's got a good chance. The restaurant that was there before didn't last too long but then I don't think they put enough effort into marketing. If the discount you've offered to the police works out then it might turnout to be quite lucrative. I hope what's his name was grateful?'

'Alec? Oh he was really pleased – should be good for the business taking off. He's a nice guy to work for and I get on quite well with him. Not to mention . . .' she stopped mid-sentence and looked a little sheepish.

Abigail looked at her curiously. 'Not to mention . . . what exactly?'

Emma was smiling now. 'One of the police who had come to try out the restaurant last night started talking to me after the, well, the incident, and he asked me out on a date.'

Abigail looked impressed. 'That was quick work; you've only been single for a few days. Do you think you're ready for taking the plunge again?'

'Probably not, but then I thought what the hell. He seemed like a really nice guy and I thought that this was maybe fate lending a hand so I took a chance. I don't really believe in karma and all that but if I hadn't walked out on John, I wouldn't be living here with you, wouldn't have gone for the job and not met Chris. As much as it still feels like there's a lot to sort out, maybe this is the world giving me a lucky break.'

'You could be right, and who are we to meddle with what the world wants?' Abigail relaxed back into her chair. 'I've often thought about why things happen but we can't control them and goodness knows I've spent a lot of time in the last year trying to figure that one out. But maybe we just have to accept it and try to move on. Have you given any more thought to what you're going to do long term?'

She shook her head. 'No ideas at the moment.'

'Well, as I said, you're welcome to stay here as long as you want. I've quite enjoyed having company in the house the last few days.'

Emma smiled. 'I would like to stay for a while if that is OK? The only thing I worry about is it's all working out so well for me it almost seems unfair, I mean you don't get much out of it. I just hope your friends, Alasdair for example, won't think I'm taking advantage?'

'Good God,' Abigail said, 'don't worry about him. Anyway as we've just agreed we can't argue with what the world wants and this would seem to be what it wants for us at the moment.' Emma smiled.

'Thanks. If it's OK then I've arranged to meet with Chris this afternoon and I was going to ask him to pick me up from here?'

Abigail nodded to indicate she had no problem. 'Of course, if you can't trust a policeman who can you trust? He seems keen anyway.'

'He does. Although with me working at the restaurant again tonight and Chris on duty at High Tea in the Park tomorrow, this was the best chance we've got this weekend.'

Abigail got up from her chair. 'I'll probably be out later as well. Speaking of not having any control over things, I need to try and keep Alasdair occupied to stop him getting into mischief.'

'Why? What's he done?'

'Oh nothing yet,' she put the dishes in the sink, 'but I need to try and keep it that way. Wait until I tell you the latest . . .'

Alasdair stood outside the black iron gates and peered through them and up the long driveway. *I wonder if he can see me just now on one of his security cameras. He might still be out or bothering my wife at the park, maybe I should have gone there first. Don't want to get in Sophie's way today though, she would not be pleased.*

Just as he was wondering whether to buzz the intercom or go up to the park after all, given that those were the only two options available to him since scaling the gates was definitely not a possible course of action, there was a crackle of electricity and a creak as the gates started to open. *Huh? Maybe my luck's in,* he thought, as he started up the drive. *If he doesn't know I'm here then I'll be able to catch him offguard and see what he's got to say for himself.*

At the front door he stood for a moment, psyching himself up. Although he was used to confrontation from his days as a solicitor, not to mention having to deal with those of a criminal nature, he was now retired and was out of the habit of this type of thing. There wasn't much call for this in his daily routine and you forgot sometimes that there was a whole world going on that you never see. People all living their lives, for good or bad, but unless you were confronted with it then you didn't see it. Yes, you might see people on the street and guess as to their circumstances, but you would never really know. Now here he was stood on the doorstep of someone they believed was involved in fairly widespread crime and it suddenly dawned on him that this might not be a one-person job. *Maybe I should wait like I agreed, after all it's not like he did anything that bad on the camera, and I did give my word to Abby. I should have thought of this before now, but then what's the worst* that could happen? And if people like me don't make a stand against people like him then where will the world be? This is a matter of principal and I'm well known for my stand on such matters. He grabbed a hold of the door knocker and rapped it forcefully three times against the door. Moment of truth, he thought.

'All arranged?' Abigail asked. Emma nodded as she came back into the lounge and watched as Abigail put her coat on and fastened it up.

'Yep, he'll be here at one.'

'Hope you have a nice time. I'm going round to see Alasdair and maybe suggest lunch to keep him occupied and out of mischief.' Emma looked slightly alarmed. 'Don't worry we won't cramp your style. I'll suggest we go outside the town so we'll be well away from the possibility of bumping into Milton Scott.'

'That's good,' Emma said relaxing again. 'I'll maybe see you later but if not I'll be back late again after work.'

'Okey doke. Have fun.' Abigail stopped at the front door to pick up yet another plastic charity bag and slot it into the rack. That's seven now, when are they ever going to come back for these? She pulled the door closed behind her and set off around to Alasdair's house. It was still dry but the clouds had come over and the day was now a little overcast, giving it a slight chill for this time of year. Not quite time for lighting a fire she thought, although the smell of lums wafting through the air clearly meant that not everyone shared her thoughts on this.

She walked up the garden path and took a quick glance inside the bay window as she passed it but there was no sign of life. She gave the doorbell a press and waited. The outer storm doors were closed which was unusual if Alasdair or Sophie were in but maybe it was just him being more security conscious now. She pressed the doorbell again and gave a knock on the door and waited for a minute but still no answer. Well that settles that then, he's out somewhere. Maybe he's off to the Marches to see if he can terrorise the carbon woman again with his ideas for a greener afterlife. I'll have a wander round and see if I bump into him in the town. She turned to leave but a movement caught her attention. A woman across the road was waving to her from inside her front door so Abigail walked over and smiled at her. 'Hello. Did you want me?' Dorothy Grey introduced herself.

'I've seen you before and since you seem to be a friend of the Mills I thought I should let you know about Alasdair.'

Abigail laughed. 'Now that's a conversation with a lot of possibilities. Anything in particular?' Dorothy ushered her into the house and into the lounge and explained her meeting with Alasdair a little over an hour ago.

'He seemed to be very upset. I hope he's not going to do anything rash. He went home but then came out again twenty minutes later and marched up the street. Do you think he's OK?' Abigail could feel the frustration grow within her again. Trust Alasdair to go off on a tangent on this rather than wait. But maybe he had just been blethering and he hadn't gone to Milton's house after all?

'I'm sure he'll be fine, he often gets a bee in his bonnet but it doesn't usually mean much. He is prone to jumping off the deep end but then calming down fairly quickly. You said that there's a camera on which you can view the park? Can I see it?' Dorothy opened up her laptop and navigated to the website.

'See, quite a good view of the whole thing. I take it you'll be going Mrs Craig?'

'Abigail, please. Yes, certainly. Will I see you there Dorothy?'

Dorothy shook her head. 'No, as I said to Mr Mills I don't really go out at all these days. But I'll be watching it on the camera here and I'll be joining in the spirit of it — I have bread and butter for my toast, a nice Marks and Spencer's roast dinner — one of those ones you pop in the oven — and a Victoria sponge to follow, and of course a nice tea to go along with it.' She smiled at Abigail. 'I do hope Mr Mills is fine.'

Abigail stood to leave. 'Yes, don't worry. Alasdair can look after himself and he always looks like he's going to get himself into more bother than he actually ends up in.' If only this were true, Abigail thought to herself. 'Thanks for letting me know. I'll see if I can find him but if not I'll speak to him later. I think Sophie is still at the park so I might go and see how she's getting on.'

Dorothy glanced over at the laptop screen. 'Yes, there she is. Nice to meet you Abigail, do call back anytime and we could maybe have some tea.' Abigail assured her she would and set off in the direction of the park. I'll go and see how Sophie's doing but maybe it's best not to mention any of this to her just now; she's got enough on her plate.

Chapter Thirty-Seven

The door opened and a squat bald man looked at Alasdair through narrow, suspicious eyes. 'What do you want?' he said in a rough voice. Alasdair couldn't be sure but this looked like one of the men he had seen through the kitchen window the other night.

'I'd like a word with Mr Scott please.'

'He's not in, go away.' The man started to close the door but Alasdair blurted out.

'I know what he's been up to.' The man paused. 'If he won't speak to me then perhaps I'll just need to go and speak to someone else – the police perhaps.' A voice echoed down the hall.

'It's alright, let him in.' The man moved aside and Alasdair could see Milton Scott walking towards him as he walked up the entrance hall. 'Mr Mills, what a pleasant surprise. Would you like to join me in the lounge?' Milton pushed open a door and gestured inside. Alasdair walked into the room a little hesitantly – he hadn't considered the fact that the heavies he had seen before might actually be here. In truth he hadn't actually considered anything before coming here, which made him wonder exactly what his detective manual would have to say about that. Still, he was here now and Milton would know fine that if anything happened to him then the police would be down on him like a tonne of bricks. *If only I had told Abigail I was coming here I'd feel a little bit more secure.* He looked around at the room he and Sophie had been in earlier this week, not quite sure what he was looking for, but then he did wonder if any of the things in here were part of the bounty from other thefts. I'm sure he wouldn't be stupid enough to keep things like that in the open, just in case, but sometimes these types of people are arrogant enough to think they're smarter than everyone else.

Milton sat down in a leather armchair. 'So, if I heard you correctly you know what I've been up to? Excuse my ignorance but what would that be exactly? That is other than helping your good wife out of a hole with the high tea event tomorrow of course.' Alasdair was starting to feel angry again, just with the sight of this man sitting there coolly being enough to make his blood rise.

'Aah yes, the great Milton Scott, all round good egg,' Alasdair paced around the room, 'but I know all about you now. I've done some checking and discovered your big secret!'

Milton looked unperturbed. 'What exactly would that be Alasdair?'

The familiar use of his name just annoying Alasdair even more. 'You're nothing but a thief, a common thief. You see we've checked and I know all about your little game. It's no coincidence that when someone puts things onto your website to be valued then, surprise surprise, they get stolen! You've got a great scheme going here haven't you. It used to be that burglars had to go around neighbourhoods and look in the windows or take a guess if there was anything worth stealing but not you, no you've got the twenty-first-century solution to that haven't you?' He didn't wait for an answer, being in full flow now. 'Anything which turns up on your website you've got a picture of, the address where it's kept and you even know if it's worth the effort to steal it. Am I on the right track, Milton?'

Milton smiled and held up his hands. 'Please go on, this is just fascinating stuff Alasdair.'

'I'm guessing that you get your goons to go and steal it then bring it back to you and you sell it on to a collector. It's a clever system but unfortunately you never figured on us digging into this did you? I knew there was something fishy about you the first time I met you and then when you told me about the hole in my slippers, then I had it confirmed! What do you think about that?' Alasdair puffed his chest out triumphantly and waited for Milton to start coming up with his ridiculous explanation. But it didn't happen. In a rather stereotypical kind of way Milton just started clapping his hands.

'That's quite incredible Mr Mills. I'm impressed. To be honest I did curse myself after you and your wife left and I realised what I'd done. I'm usually the most careful person you'll ever meet but somehow you just seemed to annoy me and I slipped up. Something which I'm sure you'll be pleased to hear you still seem to have the knack to do.'

Alasdair smiled. 'Well, wait until the police find all this out – you won't be any guest of honour then will you? You'll be disgraced and banged up in jail as well.' Alasdair strode off towards the door, expecting Milton to stop him but he just watched from his armchair. Opening the door, Alasdair was confronted by a barricade comprising of the man who opened the front door to him and another man who could have been his twin brother.

'Let me past you bloody oafs, I want to leave.' He tried to push through but the two men picked him up by his arms and carried him back into the room, before launching him onto the sofa in front of Milton. Alasdair felt his back flare with pain and he let out a yowl.

'Mr Mills,' it was Milton's turn to get up and pace the room, 'this is most inconvenient. You see I was really looking forward to tomorrow, and the fact that you seem intent on going to the police does trouble me somewhat. You see I don't really like the police, and worse still, I don't like them asking questions and looking into my affairs. Did you really think you could come around to my home and behave like this and then just walk out of the door again? I think you've been reading too many Miss Marple's and assumed I would just hold up my hands? Tell me, when you thought about this did you really imagine me saying, "Alright, it's a fair cop" or were you not that clichéd?' Milton walked over towards Alasdair with a look of anger on his face that made Alasdair recoil, or as much as was possible in his position on the sofa with his aching back. 'There's only one thing now that bothers me. Do you know what that is Alasdair?'

Alasdair shook his head warily. 'No, no idea.'

'We and us.'

Alasdair looked at him confused. 'Sorry?'

'We and us, Alasdair. If you had come to me and said that you had found out these things then I would take care of you, terrible accident that sort of thing, and then we would go on as we were. Well, obviously not quite going on as we were for you but you know what I mean. I'm a good study of people Alasdair and when I spoke to your wife earlier today there was not a hint that she thought I was out to do anything bad. In fact, I think she was more aggrieved with you more than anyone else! So, the question I would like answered now is who are we and us?' Alasdair was still looking confused but the penny was slowly starting to drop.

'It was just me, I did some checking on this and that's what I found out.'

'No, you had someone helping you and I want to know who.'

'You're wrong, there's no one else.'

Milton stood over him, his face calm but thoughtful. 'If only I believed you Alasdair. Perhaps you'll be so kind as to accept my invitation to stay while I decide what we're to do with you?'

Alasdair forced a small, pained smile. 'I don't suppose I can refuse can I?' Milton grinned back at him as the two men hoisted Alasdair up and over the back of the couch and dragged him off, shouting loudly, down into the basement.

Milton sat back down in his chair and laid his head back. If not Sophie, then who's the other person in Alasdair's double act? And the other question is, are they the Holmes or the Watson?

Abigail stood just inside the park gate with a small group of people watching the rehearsals. A string quartet was working its way through some of their repertoire, and down on the grass in front of the stage, Abigail could see Sophie with her arms folded, watching them intently. Every so often someone would come up to her and point somewhere around the park or to the stage, at which point Sophie would scratch her head and then point in the same direction and nod and then the person who had enquired of her would hurry off in that direction. Abigail watched with marvel at Sophie. This would be a big enough job if you were used to organising this sort of thing but she'd done it from a standing start. She should get the freedom of the city if she pulled this off tomorrow.

Abigail strolled into the park, not sure if she should go over and speak to Sophie or just leave her to it. She decided to go and speak to her – if for no other reason than she might be glad of someone speaking to her who wasn't asking her questions! She was just pointing someone off to the stage and then giving the thumbs up to the quartet who had finished a piece when she turned and saw Abigail approaching. Abigail waved to her. 'Hi Sophie, how are things shaping up?' Sophie let out a huge sigh, which seemed like it must exceed her lung capacity.

'Oh, you know. We're getting there. The stage and the sound system seem to be fine, it's just all the little details that everyone needs to ask about. I'm exhausted from it all.'

'I can see. You'll need a week in bed after this. Anything I can do to help since I'm here?'

Sophie glanced around. 'No, not really. I'm expecting some help from the other committee people in a bit so that should help. Have you seen Alasdair today?'

Abigail shook her head, trying to look nonchalant. 'No, not seen him. Is he not here with you?'

'Hah, you're joking! I think his nose is a bit out of joint with my doing all this so he's staying out of the way.' Abigail shook her head and started to protest but Sophie held up her hand. 'Oh I know Abigail, he's not really like that. I'm just a bit tired at the moment. I didn't see him this morning – he was still in bed when I got up and God knows what time I'll get home tonight.'

'Maybe best he's off somewhere else and not under your feet. I'll let you get on and if I catch up with Alasdair I'll tell him to get up here and give you some moral support.' She gave Sophie a quick hug around the shoulders and then said her goodbyes and walked back towards the gate. Typical, he's not even thought to come up here today to lend a hand to his wife! Wait until I get a hold of him. She walked back home and stopped at the corner as she saw Emma and a young man leaving the house and going off in the opposite direction. I could tail you two if I wanted you know, she thought, it'd be good practice to get away with following a police officer. Maybe not – I'm sure the course of true love does not run smooth when an interfering old woman follows you on your first date. I'm sure that's the extended saying. She walked slowly on and went into the house to have a relaxing seat for a while before trying to get a hold of Alasdair later in the afternoon.

'How long have you worked in the police?' Emma asked as they walked over the hill into town. She liked the look of Chris Buchan – he was taller than her five foot eight and he looked strongly built, if not particularly bulky with it. Short dark hair framed his handsome face.

'Just a couple of years really, still quite new to it all but I like it fine. I hope to get on in the police, not like some of the jobs I've had before, those weren't going anywhere. Hopefully I can end up in the CID someday – I'd love to do that.' He smiled warmly at her as he held open the door to the coffee shop. 'What about you? I guess you've not long started at the restaurant with it just opening last night?'

Emma explained the story of her moving in with Abigail and how she had stumbled into the job at The Pudding Furnace.

'I think I'll like that fine too although I'd love to do something more, I'm just not sure what it'll be yet.' They sat down at a table and ordered two coffees and Chris ordered a blueberry muffin and asked if Emma wanted anything. 'No thanks. Alec's testing out desserts at the moment so I'm his guinea pig. It's hard work but someone's got to do it.' Their coffees were brought over and they chatted about this and that, Emma's work at the restaurant and where she had lived before, what took Chris into the police and, in the main, just general conversation. Chris was quite open and seemed to be enjoying her company and likewise for Emma; she found him quite agreeable.

'Why don't you join the police?' he asked her, 'They're always looking for new recruits. I think you'd be good in the police.'

She laughed a little self-consciously. 'Do you think so? I've never given it any thought, but I guess it would be an experience.'

Chris nodded. 'Oh, it's that alright. All of human life is there, but at least you can make a difference and help to solve some crimes as well.'

'I guess, although I think that's more my Abigail's domain at the moment.' Chris looked at her somewhat confused. 'Oh, she and a friend have been trying to solve a burglary and trap who they think is the mastermind behind it all. All very dramatic. Actually I think they might be on to something but —,' she paused, 'maybe I shouldn't be telling you this. I don't think they're quite ready to tell the police,'

'I'm not working at the moment and you can't stop now – you've got me far too intrigued.'

'Well, she has a friend who was burgled recently and from what I can gather he persuaded her to get involved in trying to solve it because,' she flushed slightly, 'well, he didn't think the police were going to do anything. Anyway, they're now convinced they know who did it and it's a big national crime wave that he's involved in.'

Chris had leaned in a little. 'Was there much taken in the burglary?'

Emma laughed. 'No, only one thing although it's as daft a thing as I've ever heard - a pair of slippers!' She laughed again but Chris was looking at her quite seriously.

'Not some antique slippers by any chance? What was the name of this friend?' Emma gave him the name. 'Oh my God, that's my case. I was at his house and had to take statements. Sorry if he's a friend but I thought he was a pretty bad-natured man. When he thought I wasn't taking it seriously he had a really bad attitude towards me. I think that's why they sent me to the house, my inspector seemed to know this Alasdair Mills and they must have thought it was one for the new guy! We're not really any further forward yet – maybe you had better tell me what they've found out? I might be able to help push it through the proper channels, or at least make sure they're not putting themselves in harm's way.'

Emma was a little reluctant as she knew she had already said too much but then again it was a bit late now. She gave him the story of Abigail and Alasdair staking out Milton Scott's home and what they had found out through their research with the library. 'So why haven't they gone to the police yet? It sounds like they're pretty convinced of it all? They're not going to do something daft are they?'

'Well, I'm fairly sure Abigail won't but I couldn't really say the same for Mr Mills. He does seem to be a little unhinged at times.'

Chris sat back and sipped his coffee. 'Maybe I'll pass it on to my sergeant and see what he thinks.' Emma looked as if she were going to protest. 'No sense trying to stop me Emma, I've got to do my duty. I won't drop you in it though with Abigail, I'll make sure your name's never mentioned.' She felt slightly reassured but not entirely. The last thing she wanted when Abigail had not long ago agreed to give her a refuge was to have gone behind her back and blabbed when she wasn't supposed to.

'Thanks. I know they're planning to report it but maybe just not had the time yet.'

He smiled. 'It's fine. Anyway, we're not here to talk about your landlady and her eccentric friend. Let's talk about something different.'

Chapter Thirty-Eight

If you're going to be kidnapped, Alasdair Mills thought, this would seem to be the basement to be kidnapped in. Far from being the dank and dark basement usually associated with a kidnapping, where the victim is chained to a wall, this one was positively palatial by comparison. There was a sofa to sit on, the floor was carpeted in a mottled eggshell colour, and there was a desk and chair in one corner on which stood a large angle-poise magnifying glass with an inbuilt light, of the type used to inspect details in antiques and such like. A few shelves and cupboards were lined along one wall.

Not being one to sit and bemoan his situation, at least not at this stage, Alasdair started to have a look around and see if there was anything in the desk or cupboards which might be of use in his escape. As comfortable as this basement is, Alasdair thought, it is still a basement and I am still being held against my will by that crook upstairs. If he is in fact still upstairs and not already away swanning around town or the park, soaking up the atmosphere before tomorrow. I'll give him a bloody atmosphere alright if I can get out of here. The desk drawers were mainly empty aside from some paper, pencils and other stationary. Nothing of much use there. The shelves along the wall had a small collection of old Matchbox and Corgi cars on them, lined up facing outwards. Probably his toys from his childhood, Alasdair thought. I'll bet that's where his collecting began – it's textbook. The cupboards either side of the shelf had some books on antiques, collectables and that sort of thing and a few boxes of postcards, letters and some old coins. Alasdair ran his hands through them but again nothing particularly interesting leapt out at him. Elsewhere there were boxes with old books, clothes and the usual overspill from most people's lives that ends up in their basement or loft. He must have somewhere else in the house that he keeps all of the really good stuff. I'd love to have a good rake around the rooms upstairs but maybe first priority is trying to get out of here. He scanned around the room again to see if there was any other possible escape aside from the door at the top of the stairs but there was nothing. There had been a window in the basement but it had long ago been filled in with large stone blocks, which might have been to avoid the dreaded window tax. This is ridiculous, he can't seriously be going to keep me here, he's just trying to frighten me but it won't work.

Alasdair went up the stairs and banged his fists on the solid door, which he thought was made from oak when he was brought in but from this side it looked metallic. 'Help! Anyone there? Help!' His fists punctuated the shouts but judging by the sturdiness of the door it didn't seem to be doing any good. He was about to try again when there was the noise of a key being thrust into the lock on the other side and the door flew open. One of the heavies who had manhandled him earlier was standing in the doorway blocking out most of the light that was trying to come through, making it look somewhat like an eclipse.

'What do you think you're doing? If you don't shut up and sit down you'll regret it. Now . . .'

Alasdair looked at him contemptuously. 'Look you oversized buffoon, I demand to be released immediately. Where is your idiot boss, I can't speak to you.' He made to push his way past and through the door but the man didn't budge and simply picked him up and carried him bodily back down into the basement.

'Mr Scott's a very busy man and he's not here. You'll get out sometime soon but at least not until after everything's done tomorrow. Mr Scott doesn't want you ruining his big day, so I've to keep you on ice until it's time to deal with you.'

'"Keep me on ice" – have we moved to Chicago? And what do you mean, "deal with me?" What's going to happen to me?' The heavy bent over the sofa where Alasdair was sitting.

'I don't think you want to know. Anyway, it'll only be worse for you if you don't co-operate so I would suggest shutting it. You don't want to annoy me so we have a bad atmosphere, do you?' Alasdair refused to let this man see that he was intimidated.

'My dear man, between my back medication and your halitosis there already seems to be a bad atmosphere.' The man stood back and looked at him, sizing him up, before laughing and walking back up the stairs as Alasdair looked after him. A few moments later the heavy slammed the door shut with a loud bang.

Abigail hung up the phone and sat in the chair next to the sideboard in her hallway looking at the phone questioningly. Where is he? That's been two hours now I've been trying to get him and still no answer – he must be seeing the missed calls on his mobile so why not phone back? She walked through to the lounge and then on to the kitchen where she tidied a few items by the sink and moved things on the worktop, but something was unsettling her about all this. If Alasdair's gone round there and got into an argument with Milton Scott then who knows what might have happened. Alasdair might have murdered him or vice versa, or perhaps he discovered it was all a big misunderstanding and they're sitting in Milton's kitchen having a cup of tea and a laugh about the whole thing. I'm not really seeing the latter but the former might be a distinct possibility, Abigail thought to herself. If he won't answer his phone and he's not at home since I've checked already, then maybe I need to try and see if he's still at Milton Scott's house or if there's any sign of him there. She put her coat on to go around there and then stopped just before she opened the front door. What reason can I give for going to his door? I can't just turn up and ask if Alasdair's been around or perhaps you've murdered him and disposed of the body, Mr Scott? Oh yes please, I'll take another refill of my tea. It's not tea with the vicar I'm going to, I need to have some idea.

She paced back and forth in the hallway for a few moments trying to come up with something but her mind drew a blank. As she sat down again next to the sideboard, she saw the headscarf and sunglasses that Alasdair had given to her on their stake-out a few nights ago, and underneath those the private detective handbook which she picked up and skimmed through. Aah, OK, I need to have a disguise of some sort. She picked up the headscarf and tied it around her head like an old washerwoman and examined herself in the hall mirror. With that and the sunglasses, I think that passes muster as a disguise, she thought. Now I just need to have my story ready as to why I'm there. My car's broken down, or I'm a visitor to town and I'm lost? No, I don't like those. She looked around again trying to see if anything could inspire her, when her eyes fell on the very thing.

The strange head-scarfed woman stood on Milton Scott's doorstep thirty minutes later and pressed the doorbell. Abigail's heart was pounding – it's one thing to play at this but I've now got face-to-face contact with the suspect. It all seems a bit too real now. She pressed the doorbell again, and again and was about to turn and walk back up the driveway when the door opened and a rather brutish man stood before her. The adrenalin in her body was running too fast to realise that this was one of the men whom Alasdair had described to her being in Milton's kitchen, and there was no way for her to know this was Alasdair's captor… The heavy-set man was staring at her angrily but Abigail was not going to be deterred.

'Good evening sir, is it evening? It's always difficult to know if this still counts as afternoon or if it's evening, isn't it?' She smiled but the man was stony-faced.

'Whatever you're selling we don't want it. Go away.'

'But I'm not selling anything,' she was hunched over, trying to look much older and the dark glasses gave her a look of someone with an eye problem. 'Oh, I'm sorry sir, if I could just come in for a wee seat and I'll explain.' She bustled forward through the door and to her surprise the man stepped aside, letting her pass, seemingly taken aback by the boldness of this frail old lady. She made a bee-line for the lounge but he stepped in front of her and gestured to a chair in the hall.

'You can sit there for a minute. What do you want anyway?'

'Oh, I'm dropping off a charity bag for you to fill with clothes and leave out again for collection.'

He put a hand under her arm and tried to coax her off the chair. 'Great, leave it on the table there – you'll need to go now.' Abigail remained seated and the man clearly didn't want to force her off the chair.

'But we need to see which one you wish to donate to first.' She opened her handbag and pulled out seven plastic charity bags and spread them on the table and then looked up at him with shrewd eyes. 'I think you're an animal person, am I right?'

He was staring at her. 'What are you talking about, I thought you were just dropping off a bag?'

'Well, we found that most people would like to choose which charity they donate to so we're providing a new service to bring a range of bags, and you can choose which charity you wish to support. Dogs or cats?'

'Eh?'

'Dogs or cats? I'm getting a distinct animal sense from you Mr . . . ?' she paused waiting for his name but he clearly wasn't going to give it so she pushed on regardless. 'But we also have a couple here for the kids and also heart disease and the homeless? If I could even persuade you to take them all then you'd be helping a very needy homeless child with a heart condition and a cat.' She smiled weakly. 'Sorry, they make us say that, apparently no one will entertain anything these days without any waffle. Seemingly they had a brain-storming session at head office and this is what passed for some humorous banter I'm told. Now what can I leave with you?' The man looked down at the bags and to Abigail's surprise picked up the children's charity bag.

'If you leave this one I'll see what I can do, but no promises.'

Abigail stood up. 'Splendid, shows how much I know, I was sure you were a cat person.'

'Nah, never had any pets when I was younger, but I had my share of homes. Now, you better leave.' He opened the front door and Abigail walked out feeling quite elated. I must remember to come back for that bag next week and hand it in to the charity shop. She walked slowly down the driveway, aware that she may be being watched and so kept her old woman routine until she was out of sight. Well, that also confirms my suspicions about Alasdair. You certainly wouldn't need to be Sherlock Holmes to figure out that Alasdair had been there if he's not still there now. What she had smelled in the hallway was the vague but very distinctive smell of Mills' Balsam.

Later that evening, as Sophie was still finalising arrangements at the park, and Abigail was at home still trying to get a hold of Alasdair but realising she may need to give up for tonight, Alasdair was sitting in the basement eating a supper of Scotch eggs and some lentil soup, as Milton Scott looked on.

'I'm surprised to have Scotch eggs,' he said in between mouthfuls. 'I didn't think you were up on the latest culinary trends. I thought you'd be more of a pickled egg man myself.'

Milton smiled thinly. 'Don't try and annoy me, Alasdair. As I said, this is your last chance to tell me who your accomplice is before I sign your death warrant for tomorrow.'

Alasdair stopped and looked up 'Death warrant! You're not serious? That sounds a bit much.'

'Oh, I'm very serious. You don't think I'll just let you go after this is all over do you? Not when you can implicate me now in these thefts, never mind your abduction. No, I have a feeling there may be some sort of an accident tomorrow night; maybe you walked in front of a car in the dark and didn't stand a chance. I'm waiting, Alasdair?' Alasdair stuffed another piece of Scotch egg into his mouth.

'No chance,' he mumbled. 'I'll never talk.' All of a sudden there was the faint sound of bagpipes playing, which stopped them both. Milton reached into his pocket and pulled out a mobile phone on which the screen was flashing and the bagpipes became louder.

'Interesting ring tone,' Milton said. 'I never could stand the pipes though and this has been driving me daft all afternoon.'

'It'll be Sophie, she'll be wondering where I am.'

Milton looked at the phone and raised an eyebrow. 'Actually, no, she hasn't called you all day. But this Abigail has called you six times not counting this one now. She really seems to want to get a hold of you. Would you care to comment?'

Alasdair folded his arms, 'Nope, she's just my dentist.'

Milton laughed. 'Of course she is, but let me take another guess that maybe this is the other person in your 'we and us'? Since you don't seem to want to tell me, then I'll just need to find out for myself and then perhaps your friend Abigail will meet a similar fate; maybe you'll even have formed a suicide pact! All manner of things can befall people these days.' The phone stopped ringing and then a few seconds later made a beeping noise to indicate a voicemail had been left. Milton dialled the number and put it on speaker. Abigail's voice issued forth:

Alasdair, where the hell are you? I know you were at Milton Scott's house today as I could smell your balm when I was there but I don't know where you are now. Give me a call otherwise I'll try you again tomorrow morning. I've spoken to the police to say you're missing but they say that since you're an adult then you need to be missing for twenty-four hours before they'll do anything, since there's no suspicious circumstances. I didn't tell them the full story of course. Call me back as soon as you get this.

Milton pressed the red button and switched off the call. 'What does she mean she was here?' He looked around at his heavy, who was guarding the stair and exit from the basement. 'Do you know about this?'

'No, not really, well there was a woman here but she was dropping off a charity bag so . . .'

Milton's face went red. 'Idiot! The very person we want was right here in my house and you let her go?'

The heavy straightened his back. 'We didn't know we wanted her at that time and anyway how was I to know since we don't know what she looks like, do we?' and then after a heartbeat, 'Mr Scott?'

'No, we don't. But we will tomorrow. Sleep tight Mr Mills, tomorrow should be an interesting day.'

Chapter Thirty-Nine

Sophie tweaked the curtains as soon as she got up to have a look at the weather and was reasonably happy to see it was dry although a little cloudy overhead. I think that'll burn off by midday, she thought, we should get sun for this afternoon. It was only seven o'clock so she crept along the landing to the bathroom and slipped into the shower so as not to wake Alasdair. Having not come home until well after eleven last night, she had slept in the spare room – no point in both of them having little sleep, although she did think he would be up early this morning to see if he could lend a hand. Still, I might get on better if he's out of my way. It's a terrible thing to say but sometimes it's easier not having him under my feet although I'm sure I'm not the only wife who sometimes feels that about their husband! She dressed and walked quietly downstairs for a breakfast of cereal and toast and left a note for Alasdair on the kitchen table. She would call him later this morning before things got underway at the park and arrange to meet him for their high tea but for now he could sleep and she would head to the park to oversee things. The stalls would be going up now for the charity sales and the first of the musicians were arriving at ten o'clock so they could get themselves settled. She picked up her coat and bag and left by the back door to save opening the heavy front door and slipped around and off to the park filled with a curious feeling of excitement, trepidation and anticipation all rolled into one.

As Sophie was walking to the park, Abigail was lying awake after a restless night. She had gone to bed at eleven and then counted practically every hour pass on the clock, unable to relax or sleep soundly. She was still wondering if Alasdair had been home and how early she could call to check. If I can't get him this morning then I'll need to call the police again and then tell Sophie and that will shatter her day today. If he had just waited like we agreed then we wouldn't have a problem, if there is a problem. He might well be fine. Just out and about yesterday and lost track of the time, you know what he's like. She swung her legs off the edge of the bed and sat up – I'm going to phone now, it's not too early and if I wake him up then I can always give him a piece of my mind which will make me feel better, if not him.

She put on her dressing gown and went downstairs to the phone in the hallway and dialled Alasdair's mobile number again. Still no answer. She hung up and tried it again, just in case he was sleeping and had been groggily reaching for it when it stopped, but still no answer. This is becoming very worrying indeed, she thought, as she wandered through into the kitchen and sat down at the table trying to think what to do next.

After drinking several cups of tea and a slice of toast, Abigail went and tried the phone again with the same result. She threw the receiver down harshly into the cradle out of sheer frustration and it bounced out and onto the sideboard. 'Something wrong Abigail?' Emma was standing at the top of the stairs and started down as Abigail looked up.

'I think there might be, but I'm not really sure. I'm not entirely sure what to do about it either.'

Emma stopped at the bottom. 'Why don't we have some tea and let's have a chat about it?' They walked into the kitchen and Abigail sat at the table as Emma busied herself about the kitchen making some toast for herself and tea for them both as Abigail relayed the events of the last twenty-four hours to her.

'Oh my God, Abigail, that was absolutely mental. What if they had recognised you at the house and kidnapped you too? You shouldn't have done it by yourself, why didn't you tell me, I would have come with you?'

Abigail shrugged. 'I didn't really know what I was going to do until I did it, it just came to me and seemed like a good idea at the time. All in the spirit of the adventure. Anyway, you were off with your policeman so I didn't want to spoil it. How did you get on by the way?'

'Great, he's a nice guy. I'll probably see him at the park later, he's on duty. That is if we get there – what are we going to do about Alasdair? Does Sophie know about all of this?'

'No,' Abigail said sternly, 'and I don't want her to know unless I know for definite what's happened. She would want to call the police but I already tried that and was told it was too soon and there was no evidence. I don't want to spoil her big day if I can help it.' Emma was sitting opposite her now, eating some buttered toast with a thick layer of rhubarb jam.

'Aren't you supposed to follow your gut in this type of situation? That's what it says in the *Handbook*; I had a quick flick through it yesterday.'

'Not you as well,' Abigail tutted lifting a slice of toast. 'That book's going to be the death of us.' She took a bite of the toast and then a sip of tea as Emma did likewise. 'The trouble is,' she said finally, 'is that my gut instinct says he's at Milton Scott's house. If Milton has the brass neck to kidnap him in the first place I think he might well have kept him there rather than risk him being seen outside. I smelled him while I was there . . .'

'You smelled Milton Scott?'

'No, Alasdair, I smelled Alasdair and his back stuff. It'll be lingering around that house for days now, you can't get rid of it, it creates its own atmosphere wherever it goes.' She paused again for more tea before going on. 'We know that Milton Scott is guest of honour at the park today so he'll be out of the house, right?' Emma nodded in agreement. 'So maybe we need to try and use that time to see if we can liberate Alasdair from the house, or at least gather some evidence that he's there. If we can let Milton Scott think that we're in the park and he's got his attention focused there, then it might leave us an opportunity at his house. What do you think?'

'It might work I suppose,' she sounded doubtful, 'but how do we let him know, we can't exactly call him up and say "Hello, can you make sure you're out of the house for a while", can we?'

Abigail grinned excitedly. 'Why not? That's exactly what we could do.' She almost ran back out to the hall and Emma followed after her and watched as Abigail picked up the phone and hit redial. She looked at Emma and put a finger to her lips.

'Hi Alasdair, it's Abigail again. I wish you'd call me back so I know you're OK. I just wanted to let you know that I'll meet you at the park at two o'clock this afternoon as planned. I'll have the folder with all our evidence in it and we can walk up to the police station from there. See you then, I'll just be in the main arena in front of the stage.' She hung up the phone and let out a huge breath. 'My God, that was exciting.' Emma was looking on in amazement. 'Abigail, I'm impressed. I never knew you had this in you. But one question, what if he doesn't have Alasdair's phone?'

'Well,' said Abigail casually, 'if he doesn't then one of two things will happen. Either nothing will happen, or Alasdair will show up in which case he'll be in big trouble. But on the other hand, if Milton does have Alasdair's phone then . . .' she stopped as she heard her mobile phone beep from the lounge and they went through. 'Ah hah, text message from Alasdair's phone.' She read the message aloud: '*Abigail, Alasdair here. That sounds fine I'll see you there at two.*' She glanced at Emma as she put down the phone. 'Perfect.'

In the basement at Milton Scott's house, the man in question was sitting on a chair opposite Alasdair on the couch and he had an unbearably smug look on his face. 'Well, it looks like it'll be easier than I thought to meet your friend Abigail.' Alasdair looked shaken from hearing the message and listening to Milton dictate the text aloud as he typed.

'You better not harm her or I'll . . .'

Milton laughed and stood up. 'You'll what? You'll not do anything since you'll be sitting tight with your bodyguard here.' He looked at his heavy by the stairs. 'You can stay here with our guest – your brother and I will go to the park and sort out this Abigail woman.'

Chapter Forty

Abigail and Emma passed the morning as constructively as they could but something was nagging at them both and it was Emma who voiced it first, 'Abigail? What if you were at the park and played along with whatever happens? Wouldn't that look better and give more time at the house to get Alasdair? I mean if Milton Scott realises quite quickly that you're not there then he might get suspicious and phone whoever might be at the house and alert them?'

Abigail's mouth thinned. 'I'd been thinking along the same lines but I don't see what can be done, I can't be in two places at the same time. I've got the perfect cover to go back to the house as I can say I'm picking up the charity bag I left yesterday. Then when they go to get it I'm hoping I can get inside and have a look around, or if not maybe even break-in through the back. Not sure, but ...'

'I'll go.'

Abigail stared at her. 'What? I don't think so ...'

'But it makes perfect sense. He's never met you before so he doesn't know what you look like or how old you are so I could easily pass myself off as you, at least long enough to buy you some time. Come on Abigail, I want to do something.'

Abigail watched her closely – this was getting out of hand. This wasn't supposed to happen, getting everyone involved in this business, especially someone that didn't really have to be involved.

But then again, going to the park wouldn't be that dangerous; it was a public place with plenty of people around and it would be a good idea to have some cover there.

'OK then, but you have to do as I say and stay in public places and no heroics, understand?'

Emma let out a small shriek of excitement. 'Anything, God this will be fantastic.'

Abigail watched her race out of the lounge and upstairs to change. Well at least she's happy which would appear to be an unexpected bonus, she thought.

Alasdair looked at his watch and saw that the time was one thirty. I've been here for almost a whole day now, he thought. Not sure I like this kidnapping business, the time really draws out and makes it a long day. Still, at least I've been fed and watered and he's not just abandoned me in the cellar. I wonder if Soph's phoned the police about me not coming home last night. If not then she'll be busy now looking after things at the park; it'll be in full swing now. But she must have noticed I didn't come home, surely? Although with everything going on we could have missed each other between rooms. I wish I'd helped her a bit more with all the planning rather than just trying to take over like I always do. She's a saint putting up with me sometimes and it's about time that I started to appreciate it a little more. It's funny how a near-death experience can make you examine things and see them more clearly. Speaking of which, I still don't know exactly how near death my experience is at the moment. He said he would keep me until things were all done today which could give me about seven hours but then what if he changes his mind? For all I know he could have changed his mind and his goons are on their way here to sort me out at any moment. He heaved himself up from the sofa and walked around the room looking at everything again, trying to see if there was something that he could use for a weapon. Why is it that there's never a stray wrench or hammer left lying around or even a big lump of wood – kidnappers always leave something like that around in the afternoon films on television but not, it would seem, in reality. Maybe I could hit them with a chair or this big magnifying glass, although they're not the easiest things to swing over my head and with the size of those men it might just bounce off them anyway. No, it needs to be something with a bit more impact. He paced around the desk and back across to the sofa and plonked himself down, looking all the time for something. Come on Alasdair, he chided himself, you're a bright man, you've got to think of something. His eyes wandered the room again before falling on some small objects and he smiled. Of course, he thought, it's child's play.

Chapter Forty-One

Sitting in the car, parked a discrete distance across the street from the park, Abigail and Emma looked on as High Tea in the Park got into full swing. Emma wound down a window and they could hear the classical music drifting across, and in the arena a sizeable crowd was watching the stage. Almost as many people again were sitting in the marquees enjoying their cakes, toast or whichever course they were on. 'It looks really something doesn't it,' she said, 'especially with the castle in the background.'

Abigail had been sitting silently. 'It does. I'm still not sure this is a good idea you know, are you sure you want to do this?'

Emma sighed. 'We've been through this and we're here now so I would just do it anyway when you left to go to Milton's house so there's no point even discussing it.'

Abigail put a hand on to Emma's. 'Just be careful, that's all I'm saying.' She smiled. The music stopped and Emma looked down at the schedule she had for the day's events.

'Looks like there's an American band on next, playing film and TV themes, which should be good. At least I'll get to see them while I'm over there. Shouldn't we get into position, as they say?' Abigail nodded and they both got out of the car with Emma walking over to the park as Abigail walked down the road towards Milton Scott's house, her head covered in the dreaded headscarf, wearing her sunglasses and affecting her now customary stoop which went with this disguise.

Emma walked into the park by the main gate past the Victorian drinking fountain and stood for a moment surveying the scene in front of her. The crowd of people seemed to be mostly around the sides of the arena, which had been roped off, and were either up close to the stage or perusing the stalls along the outer edge. *If he's going to see me anywhere then it'll be right in the middle of the grass there.* She was carrying a buff folder with her which was padded out with various pieces of paper and some old pages from a newspaper which they had cut up before they left, to give the authentic look of a folder filled with incriminating evidence. Emma had wanted to actually write the word 'EVIDENCE' on it in black marker but Abigail had quite rightly suggested that they might as well put the word 'ACME' on there as well if they were going to do that. The reference was somewhat lost on Emma at first but the cartoon quality of it was explained by Abigail.

She walked as casually as she could, since her nerves were jangling a little now, and stood in the middle of the grass and turned around in a circle. Trying not to look too suspicious just seemed to be making her feel even more suspicious. Five minutes became ten and the band on the stage was playing the theme tune from *Jaws* now, the low bass of the opening rumbling across the park. Just as she was thinking she might have to move onto somewhere else, a voice behind her made her jump.

'Good afternoon Abigail.' She turned and saw a thirtyish-year-old man, whom she didn't find particularly handsome even with his expensive suit. He was smiling at her. 'I see you have your folder with you. Waiting for someone in particular?' Emma's mind had gone blank when he had spoken but she suddenly remembered that she was meant to be Abigail.

'Erm, yes actually. I'm meeting someone here shortly. Sorry I can't talk.' She turned around and held her breath waiting to see what he did next. Even with all the people milling around, she still felt her heart pounding in her chest with fear.

'There's no need to be rude Abigail, after all we do have a mutual friend in Alasdair Mills, don't we?' She turned around again and he was standing closer now, his breath smelling of jam, fish and cream all at once. He's had his high tea then, she thought.

'Oh, you know Alasdair do you? How come?'

He was smirking. 'Come on now, we're not going to play this game are we? You know who I am and I know exactly why you're here. Something to do with that quite jam-packed folder under your arm. Why don't I take that from you and we can go somewhere to discuss things?'

She gripped the folder. 'No, I'm fine here thanks.' As she said this she felt a strong hand grip her arm and a smell of sweat and beer filled her nostrils. She tried to wriggle her arm free but it was being held fast and, turning her head, she could see a huge hulk of a man now standing behind her gripping onto her.

The smile had left Milton Scott's face and his eyes were piercing. 'Don't make a sound or it'll be the last thing you do, I swear. Now, give me the folder and come with us.' He reached for the folder and slid it from under her arm and was just about to open it when a voice rang out across the park.

'Milton?' He forced a smile onto his face and looked over Emma's shoulder, past his accomplice, and towards the sound of the voice. 'Milton, there you are, we need you for judging the cream cake contest in the main tent.' Sophie walked over to where they stood and looked at them all curiously, holding her hand out to Emma. 'Hello, Sophie Mills, nice to meet you.' Emma's head was spinning and Milton's face was looking wrought with confusion.

He let out a snorting, almost nervous laugh. 'Sophie, you know this person don't you? Abigail Craig?'

Sophie looked at him. 'Oh, this isn't Abigail, although I'm sure Abigail would love to be this young again!' Milton's face briefly took on a confused expression but then erupted with anger and he ripped open the folder and saw the random pieces of paper inside which fluttered into the breeze as he scrabbled through them, 'You . . .' He looked as if he was about to hit Emma but stopped short. 'Back to the house, now!' The large man behind

Emma released her arm and he and Milton raced off towards the gate. Emma felt in a state of shock but was still able, rather bizarrely, to register that the music now was the theme tune to *Chariots of Fire*.

Chapter Forty-Two

In the basement of Milton Scott's house, Alasdair let out a huge yell of pain and rolled on the floor clutching his chest. He could only hope that the sound would travel far enough through the heavy door at the top of the stairs and into the house for Milton's heavy to hear it. He was sure that Milton would be at the park by now as planned, since there was no way he was going to miss his big day in the spotlight, and only one of his heavies would be in the house now. He let out another howl of agony and rolled onto his back crying out again for good measure. This time he heard the key clanking into the lock and the door opened and the heavy appeared. 'What the hell is all the noise about? Get up and keep quiet or I'll give you something to shout about.' Alasdair rolled over again and clutched his chest even tighter and shouted back breathlessly.

'Help me, I think I might be having a heart attack, please!' He wondered if his performance was perhaps a little too over the top, it certainly wasn't going to win him an Olivier award, but it seemed to have worked in getting some attention anyway. He rolled about on the floor but sneaked a look to the top of the stairs and saw the heavy start to run down. He was on the fifth step when his foot slid out from under him and a Ford Capri car shot off the stairs from underneath his foot. A split second after that his other foot landed on top of a small Austin Metro which shot down the stairs as he tried to grab onto the wall, but his hands just slipped on the smooth surface and he flailed helplessly. They say that in moments like these things go in slow motion but from Alasdair's point of view it was anything but, as the huge man fell with a resounding crunch and crumpled down the stairs. The man started rolling around on the floor in agony as Alasdair hauled himself up using the sofa and ran, veering around him and going up the stairs. He stopped at the top and looked back to see his captor get to his feet and look somewhat groggily up at him, but before he could make a move Alasdair stepped through the door and slammed it shut behind him, locking it quickly. Just as he was looking around the hallway he heard the loud doorbell chime and was suddenly thrown into a panic. It could be help, he thought quickly, but it could just as easily be someone in on this whole thing. I better hide in case they come in.

Abigail pressed the doorbell again as she knew someone must be in as she could hear a door closing and then footsteps beyond the front door. But no answer came from inside. Chancing her arm, she pressed down on the handle and it clicked open, so she pushed the door inwards and saw the empty hallway. Oh dear me, she thought sarcastically, the door has opened all by itself – I better check everything is OK inside. She walked into the hallway and looked first into the lounge door but there was no one there. Then she went across and opened another door which seemed to be a home cinema room, with an array of sofas arranged in a semi-circle facing a large television mounted above the fireplace. Nice, she thought, closing the door again to move on with the search. She was about to go into what would be the kitchen when she heard a noise from behind another door across the hallway; a sort of groaning sound was emanating through the door. She threw off her stoop and nimbly crossed the hall to the door. 'Alasdair? Is that you? Are you OK?' Only a loud groan answered her. Oh my God it must be him, they've tied him up or been torturing him or goodness knows what. She noticed the large key in the lock and turned it, heaving open what was a heavier door than she was expecting. She looked inside and down the stairs to see a huge bald-headed man sitting on a sofa and looking up at her, rubbing his back and groaning. He let out a guttural yell and started getting to his feet. Abigail ran back out into the hallway, looking around frantically, 'Alasdair?' she yelled at the top of her voice, 'Are you here? It's Abigail!' Over the grunting coming up the stairs behind her she heard a familiar shout from the main stairs in front of her.

'Abby?' she turned and saw Alasdair descending the stairs. 'Thank God it's you; I thought I was in for it. I managed to escape and lock the bloody great oaf in the basement.' He gestured over to the door and saw it lying open. 'Did you open that?' Abigail nodded in a state of bewilderment. 'What the hell did you do that for?' He raced towards her, somewhat impaired by his now throbbing back, as a giant shadow appeared at the door. 'Come on!'

They did their best attempt at a run for the front door, slamming it behind them and making their way as quickly as they could manage down the drive to the main road. They heard the front door open behind them and another yell from the direction of the house.

Abigail's mind was racing. 'Let's get to the park, there are lots of people there so we'll be safe. We can get the police while we're there.' They turned right outside the gate and made an attempt at a run again towards the park, which was about five hundred yards away. Alasdair was almost bent over with the pain in his back.

'This is a bloody irony, I hope they think it's funny putting the *Chariots of Fire* music on. Is this meant to inspire me to run faster!?

'Oh stop moaning, come on.' They made it about a hundred yards when, looking up ahead, they saw the familiar figure of Milton Scott running towards them with the double of the man who was behind them. Abigail and Alasdair stopped, trying to figure the best way to go but in doing so allowed the heavy behind them to gain enough ground to effectively cut them off from going anywhere. In front of them, Milton and the other heavy slowed to a walk, an angry look on Milton's face as he approached them.

'You think you're so bloody smart don't you, sending that girl to the park. Well, your luck's run out now. Get them!' He waved his arms in their direction and the two heavies moved in to grab them both. As they felt huge arms engulf them in bear-like grips, a car screeched to a halt next to them with another following behind.

'Let them go now! Police!' a voice shouted and four police officers came running towards them.

Milton Scott held up his hands. 'Thanks goodness you're here officers, I'd like to make a complaint. These two broke into my house . . .' He stopped with a yell of complaint as his arms were pulled behind his back and handcuffed. Abigail recognised the young man as Chris Buchan. Emma must have alerted him at the park. She suddenly had a dreadful thought. 'Chris, where's Emma, is she OK?' Chris was puffing as he handed Milton over to one of his colleagues, who took him away and into the back of one of the police cars. His two accomplices were already in one of the other cars, having decided to come quietly, much to the relief of the officers involved.

'She's fine; she's still at the park. Are you two OK, that's more to the point?' Alasdair was about to open his mouth when Abigail cut him off.

'We're fine.' Alasdair looked at her incredulously.

'You might be fine, but I've been held hostage for twenty-four hours. I'm in a state of trauma!'

'Yes, you look it.' She looked back to Chris, 'What happens now?'

'Well, we'll take these three to the police station and I would suggest that we get you checked out at the hospital, just as a precaution, then we'll get you to the station to give statements.

Our scenes of crime people will be having a good look around Mr Scott's house very shortly.'

Abigail waved her hand. 'I'm fine. I want to go and see Emma. Alasdair you should go you've been . . .'

He waved his hand as well. 'I want to see Sophie. Does she know anything about all of this?' Abigail shook her head but Chris chipped in.

She does now, she was there when Emma was rumbled and then called me.'

Abigail and Alasdair walked slowly up to the park as the police cars turned and moved off. They could hear the theme tune to *Rocky* playing now from the park.

'That's more like it,' Alasdair said as they neared the park gate. 'Thanks for that, Abby. I would have been OK you understand but I appreciate you coming to get me. How did you know I was there?' She looked at him and raised an eyebrow.

'I just followed my nose,' she said, walking into the park.

Chapter Forty-Three

Abigail was the first to arrive at The Pudding Furnace on Monday night and Emma greeted her warmly and showed her over to a nice booth facing the fire. 'It's a pity it's not lit, Abigail, this place will be so cosy in the winter.'

Abigail looked around at the other tables. 'Quiet tonight isn't it?'

'It's early yet but then Monday's never a busy night for restaurants. Whose idea was it to book the table for six o'clock?'

'Oh, Alasdair of course. I booked it for seven thirty but he changed it to six, as he doesn't want to be eating too late. He wants to get home for some more recuperation. I bet he'll do a fair bit of recuperating tonight when he sees the selection of whiskies behind the bar.'

Emma laughed. 'I'd better go, other customers to see to.' She whisked off and went to another table with a young couple and a small child. The child, a boy of around six years old, was eating a pie of some description and some vegetables. Very good, Abigail thought, none of this kid's menu nonsense which everyone seems unable to do without these days. Grown-up food was good enough when I was young so it should be good enough now. She was at the point of being very impressed when there was a slight coming together of knife and fork which sent a flotilla of peas sailing across the table. The boy's mother looked around and saw Abigail watching but she just smiled and then set to putting things right. Abigail smiled back, impressed at such a well-behaved child.

Sometimes she thought that was a rarity but in fact she was sure there were lots of well-behaved children. The ones that visited the library were, for the most part, very well behaved and most seemed even to have mastered the concept of silence, as long as it was for a short-enough period.

The restaurant door opened and a small bell chimed above it causing Abigail to look over. Alasdair stood there holding a bunch of flowers. 'Hi Abby, here we are again!'

'What have you done to Sophie now?' Abigail asked, incredulous that he might have upset her again within a week.

He laughed. 'Ha, nothing at all. She's just parking the car over the road.' As he was taking his coat off Sophie walked in and Emma took both of their coats and they sat down, Alasdair sliding into the booth first, with Sophie nudging him to budge up a bit.

'Hi Abigail, how are you feeling? Did you get on OK with the police?'

Abigail nodded. 'Oh fine, yes, just gave my statement and told them everything we'd done, well almost everything. You did remember to leave out the bit about the library van, didn't you?' she said to Alasdair, who nodded distractedly as he studied the menu. 'And then they said that was it. We'll be needed as witnesses when it goes to court but that won't be for some time. How about you?'

Alasdair shrugged. 'Much the same Abby, much the same. I was given a bit of a lecture for putting myself into harm's way and getting myself kidnapped but other than that it was fine. Speaking of which, we got these for you,' he handed the flowers to Abigail, 'as a thank you for helping with everything. I'm not saying that I wouldn't have solved it by myself but it was good to have someone assisting me.'

'Assisting you?' Abigail exclaimed.

'Oh pay no notice to him Abigail,' Sophie cast him a cold glance, 'he's just annoyed because it was more you that solved it than him. Did the police give you any more details of what had been going on?'

'A few, although Emma managed to get some information from her new boyfriend, this Chris Buchan. He's likeable enough I think and she seems keen on him. Anyway, it appears that Milton Scott was using his website to generate sales leads, if you like, for where there were things worth stealing. Then he was almost operating a franchise system for burglary around the country. He couldn't cover everything himself with just his two cohorts so he had sent them to make contact with local burglars and if they did the work they would get a cut while the rest of the money came back to Milton. Quite enterprising really when you think about it, just a pity it was all criminal. Chris said that the computer forensics people are going over the equipment they seized from his house but they think they can probably link about thirty burglaries back to him, either directly or by tying up the items stolen with those on his website. It was so spread out that no one had put two and two together previously, until I —,' Alasdair looked at her, 'sorry, we,' she smiled, 'pulled in the information from all of the other library people.'

Sophie was smiling. 'It's been quite an adventure, and while I can't say I was overly enamoured with it all this last week while I was trying to get the high tea up and running, now that it's out of the way I'm starting to come around to the excitement of it all.'

Alasdair harrumphed next to her. 'I'll be more excited when I get my slippers back. The police say I can't get them back until after the trial as they'll be held as evidence. Can you believe it?'

Abigail nodded. 'Of course I can believe it. You didn't think you'd get them back straight-away did you? You need to read that last couple of chapters of your book again.' She turned to Sophie. 'So how did the day go? Was a lot of money raised for charity?'

'About ten thousand pounds – enough that they might let us do it all again next year. We'll see, depends on the council coffers I suppose. But I had my guest of honour for the closing speech didn't I?'

Alasdair feigned shyness. 'Oh it was nothing, just the least I could do to show my appreciation for my darling wife.' Abigail had to admit that Alasdair's closing speech had been lovely. Since Milton was otherwise detained, he had been drafted in and had spent most of the time dedicating the event to Sophie and making sure she got a huge round of applause from the audience, who for their part also cheered loudly.

Emma came over to the table and took their orders and disappeared back to the bar. As she did so, Alec came out from the kitchen and spoke to her quietly before coming up and introducing himself.

'Aye, it was a great day all round,' he said. 'Those that hadn't quite had enough to eat must have come into town. We were packed in here last night.' Emma came over, clinking a bucket of ice out of which poked a bottle of champagne. 'Just me wee way of saying thank you and congratulations on your success.' The three of them looked a little embarrassed but, thankfully, Alec made his excuses and returned to the kitchen to work as Emma popped open the champagne and poured out the glasses.

'Well,' said Alasdair, holding up his glass, 'here's tae us. Wha's like us? Not many and they're aw' dead.' They clinked their glasses together and took a sip, the bubbles nearly catching Abigail.

'Here here! Oh, I could get used to this. We need to do this more often.'

Sophie nudged Alasdair. 'Did you tell Abigail about the tickets?'

He gasped at his forgetfulness. 'My God no, I forgot. Abby, you'll love this – we've all got tickets to go to a grand dinner at the castle in a few months. It's a big deal, black tie and all that, to celebrate part of the castle opening up again. What do you say?'

Abigail pondered it for a moment. 'Well, I did vow to try and avoid any events with you two in the near future, given how yesterday went,' she laughed, 'but of course. I mean a dinner at the castle, not much can happen there . . . ?